Goldie. 

Goldie.

Stacey Pyne

Goldie
Published by Stacey Pyne
New Zealand
Instagram: stacey_pyne

© 2020 Stacey Pyne

ISBN 978-0-473-50765-7 (Softcover)
ISBN 978-0-473-50766-4 (ePUB)
ISBN 978-0-473-50767-1 (Kindle)

Editing:
Iola Goulton & Andrea Candy

Illustration:
Milla Pyne

Production & Typesetting:
Andrew Killick
Castle Publishing Services
www.castlepublishing.co.nz

Cover Design:
Stephen Kirkby
hi@parkbyprojects.com

For my loves.
Jake. Milla. Hayes. Ari.

Prologue

As a child, she would read through his stories and, like seeds, they took hold of her heart.

'Thank you for your words,' she would tell him. 'I love your stories.'

She wondered about the unseen characters. About the unheard voices.

What were *their* stories?

What did they see, hear, think and taste?

Taking form in the dark, like treasure, over time the seeds grew.

Until one day they began to escape through her fingertips and, slipping out onto fresh white paper, Goldie was born.

'I love your stories,' she would tell him.

'*I love yours too,*' he replied.

Asher

The room was finished. Asher could hardly believe it. Standing in the doorway, he scanned the space from one corner to the other. It was perfect. He'd worked on the wooden floors for a solid month. Sanding, polishing, perfecting. Now they shone from their final varnishing. The large oak table running down the centre of the room was a masterpiece, something any craftsman would be proud to have created. And he'd created it. He stepped forward and ran his fingers along the grain of the wood, breathing in the scent of fresh polish.

He'd stayed up to an unearthly hour the night before, the familiar tugging in his spirit calling him to clean the room. He'd dusted every corner from ceiling to floorboards. He'd gone over every crevice in the wooden chairs, wiping away sawdust and fingerprints. He couldn't stop, wouldn't have been able to sleep, until it was complete.

Asher had inherited the family home last year, after his father passed away. It had been a time of grief, loss and adjustment. He'd wandered aimlessly around his home for months mourning for his father.

He'd climbed up the stairs one morning, as he so often did, making his way to the rooftop. But he'd stopped at the doorway to the guest room. He hadn't paid it much attention in the past. Stepping into the room, it was obvious it hadn't been used in years. After Asher's mother had died, his father had struggled to keep up with the house alone.

Asher had stood in the doorway, thinking fondly of his parents and how they had been so different to this dark lifeless room, when he'd seen what could only be described as a vision. The air was stale and dust filled the room, but he'd imagined it revived, bought to life and full of purpose. Where there was a sleeping mat and a dusty old storage cabinet, Asher saw pristine, polished wooden floorboards and a large dining table set for entertaining. He'd looked at the small window hidden beneath a faded curtain laced with spiderwebs with barely a trace of light piercing through. In its place he'd seen a large light-filled window with sunshine flooding into the space.

He'd been deeply stirred, hardly able to sleep through the night in anticipation of getting started. Something within him urged him on, giving him a sense that he must begin the work. He decided not to think about it too much. He didn't know what he was preparing the room for, or even if it would ever be admired or enjoyed. But there was no mistaking the whispering in his spirit as he worked.

A few weeks into the project, Asher had shared his plans with Zac. That had been a mistake. His childhood friend, the one constant in his life, had laughed and called Asher an idiot for spending his hard-earned coin on a guest room.

'Asher, in all the years I've known you, you've never entertained visitors in your home or had someone stay the night.' Zac punched him in the shoulder. 'You should've come and built me an expensive guest room with a dining table. You know I'd have put it to good use.'

Asher knew Zac had been joking. But he also knew Zac was right. Asher was an introvert who preferred to keep to himself, while Zac was the life of the party. He and Zac had always been polar opposites.

But that familiar tug had been there the following morning, stronger than the day before, urging him to continue with his work in the guest room. He couldn't have stopped even if he'd wanted to. His hands and feet seemed to know a secret he hadn't been let in on.

Now Asher headed for the front door, his empty water pitcher in hand, when he was struck with a thought. The box of treasures! He placed his pitcher beside the door and headed for the storeroom in his courtyard, excitement rising within him. He couldn't believe he'd forgotten the treasures. Asher's mother had inherited them from an aunt who was quite the entertainer.

If he remembered correctly, the box was full of copper and bronze tableware. He reached back behind a tall stack of fabric and found the box he'd never expected to have a use for. He'd only kept it in case he got into a fix and needed some fast coin. But now he was excited with the idea of setting his beautiful new table. He placed the box on the floor, opened the lid and smiled. This would be perfect.

Asher carried the forgotten treasure to the guest room. He was pleased to discover a large embroidered table cloth beneath the dishes. It was folded carefully, no doubt to protect the precious contents. He shook the linen cloth out and spread it across the table. It fit like a glove. There was a peaceful presence in his room today with a gentle breeze blowing the new curtains and sunlight pouring into the room.

An hour later, Asher stood back admiring his handiwork. The copper and bronze was something else, setting the room off to perfection. It was a shame no one else would enjoy it. The thought was discouraging. He took one last look at the space he'd created and closed the door. The room was complete now. He walked slowly down the stairs and headed to the town well with his water pitcher.

Asher filled his pitcher at the well in the centre of town. He couldn't help feeling down. He knew his room was finished, but restoring the room had been his life for many months. Had he wasted his time? Was his deep belief that his efforts were somehow part of a bigger plan a foolish mistake, like Zac had said?

Asher walked home slowly, scuffing his sandals along the dirt as he went. He thought about dropping in to Zac's but decided against it. He would see him later for the Passover meal anyway.

As he turned in to his street, he heard a noise behind him. He looked over his shoulder. Two men were behind him. They were dressed simply and chatting. Asher hadn't seen them in his neighbourhood before. They must be visiting one of his neighbours for Passover.

The water pitcher was growing heavy by the time he arrived home. He stepped inside and placed it with relief on the table. There was a knock at the door. It was the two men from the road.

'Can I help you?' Asher asked.

'Yes, please,' one of the men replied with a smile. 'Can we speak to the owner of the house?'

'You're speaking to him.' Why did they want to know?

'Great.' The man's tone was positive, but he looked nervous. The stranger glanced back to his friend, who stood further back on the doorstep. Should Asher be worried? Were the men dangerous? They seemed harmless enough, but what did they want? He had no idea.

'The Teacher asks: "Where is the guest room where I can eat the Passover meal with my disciples?"' The man looked Asher square in the eyes. His words held an authority that wasn't there before, as though he'd remembered something, as though his words were not his own.

Asher stared at the men, his mind blank. He couldn't speak and he couldn't believe what he'd just heard. Surely they didn't mean his guest room? How could these men have known about his project? Was this some sort of trick? Was Zac playing with him?

As he looked at each of them, it was clear they were serious.

'The Teacher' … the familiar tug in his spirit pushed him forward. Tears pricked his eyes as he ushered them inside. They looked as surprised as he was as they removed the sandals from their feet. Asher took the lead, full of amazement and wonder.

The two strangers followed him up the stairs to his guest room.

'Where do you want us to prepare it?' they asked him.

He replied, 'As soon as you enter Jerusalem, a man carrying a pitcher of water will meet you.

'Follow him. At the house he enters, say to the owner, "The Teacher asks: Where is the guest room where I can eat the Passover meal with my disciples?" He will take you upstairs to a large room that is already set up. That is where you should prepare our meal.' (Luke 22:9-13)

The Cry

The cry came from somewhere deep down within, from a place where pain ran heavy and desperation was raw. Formed in the lungs, it began its journey. Travelling up and weaving through vocal cords and then out of parted lips – where it took off on the wind. And was carried through time and space, through light and deep darkness and into the great unknown. Into the place where mercy is birthed. And further still, seeking the heart of all things. Until it floated up the side of a golden throne and found its resting place – inside of his ear.

But in my distress, I cried out to the Lord; yes, I prayed to my God for help. He heard me from his sanctuary; my cry to him reached his ears. (Psalm 18:6)

Mara

Day One

Mara lifted her head from her hands and looked out to the distant mountains. It had been another long night without Levi.

The memories were relentless. She was drowning in them. No longer able to lie still, she'd moved to sit by the window and let the tears come.

It was four months since Levi died. Mara hadn't talked to God since. Maybe she never would.

The town of Nain slept around her. Four-year-old Ikee was tucked in her bed. He'd slept with her since the accident.

She reached her arms above her head and stretched her fingers high. She needed to sleep. She tiptoed back across the floor and slid in beside her son.

It had been a hot summer and his hair had grown light in the sun. He was so like Levi with his olive skin and full lips.

Mara planted a kiss on the tip of Ikee's nose, then lay down next to him, foreheads almost touching. She closed her eyes.

Too soon, she was woken by his little body lying on her torso. She opened her eyes and found herself looking down his throat.

'Aaahhhhhh. Can you see that Mama?' he asked.

Mara yawned.

'What is it, Ikee? she asked.

'It's an ouchy, Mama.'

Mara lifted her head off the pillow.

'Is it hurting?' She kept her voice calm. Ever since Levi's death, she'd panicked over the slightest thing. She couldn't lose Ikee as well.

'It's an ouchy in my mouth, Mama.'

'Let me sit up, so I can have a proper look' She lifted him under his arms and sat him on her lap.

Everything looked fine, but that wouldn't stop her from visiting Beth, the healer, again.

Ikee skipped along the road in front of Mara. He seemed cheerful enough but she couldn't be too careful. They had developed a routine since Levi's death. Breakfast, then work at the fruit stall, then home for dinner and bed. If Mara stuck to the routine, she could make it through the day without him.

Beth took one look at Ikee jumping around and smiled at Mara. Mara felt her cheeks redden.

'Ikee complained of a sore throat…' Now her son was jumping from one stool to another, squealing with delight.

She was thankful that Beth led him to the bed anyway. She looked him over.

'Ikee, have you been a good boy for your Mama?'

Ikee nodded, his wee head bobbing up and down.

'I picked Mama flowers,' he said. His eyes were fixed on the sweet jar in the corner.

Beth ruffled his hair and winked at Mara.

It was a long day at the fruit stall. Ikee had fallen asleep under a table stacked high with dates. It was unusual for him – he never slept in the day.

Mara wished he didn't have to spend his days at the stall

but Ikee didn't seem to mind. He made friends everywhere he went.

Mara had been desperate for work after Levi's death. She'd paced the stalls back and forth, clutching Ikee's hand in her own. When she'd spotted Old Paddy stooping down to retrieve fallen fruit and then struggle to get back up, Mara had sat Ikee down and told him to wait there.

'Mama's going to get us a job. It will be fun.' She'd tried to sound convincing.

But by the time Mara had arrived inside the fruit stall, Ikee had jumped off his perch, made his way in the side entrance and was already speaking with Paddy. Mara hid and listened. Why had Ikee disobeyed her the minute she'd taken her eyes off him?

'What are you doing young man?' she heard Paddy ask. 'I don't want any trouble now, you hear me?'

'My mama is getting us a job here, it will be fun,' Ikee told him and Mara winced. 'I have to sit there.' He pointed to the curb. 'Can I have an apple while I wait?' Mara smiled to herself. Ikee had always had a soft spot for apples.

Paddy looked surprised.

'Is she just? We'll see about that won't we?' He grunted at Ikee. 'And no, you cannot have an apple.'

Mara had intervened then and explained their situation to Paddy, who had taken pity on them, much to her surprise. Paddy had lost his wife earlier that year and Mara wondered if he was lonely. Paddy had given Ikee an apple that day and each day since.

Day Two

The morning was grey, but Mara had finally slept. Ikee was still asleep.

That was unheard of – he was usually up at the crack of dawn. She rolled over. He was sleeping soundly, his tiny lips slightly parted. Oh, how she loved him. At times like this, she would thank God for him. She'd been close to God once, but not now.

She held her hand over Ikee's but drew back when she felt his warmth. His hand was burning.

Was something wrong?

She sat up and tried to remain calm. She took a deep breath and told herself she was overreacting… again. Ikee was fine. He had to be fine.

She held her hand on his brow. Her heart sank. He was too warm. She'd have to wake him and go to Beth's.

Mara whispered to him. She whispered quietly at first, then a little louder, then louder still.

But Ikee wouldn't wake up.

She had to get him to Beth, fast. She lifted him from the bed, and he lay still in her arms. She ran from her house, his heart beating against hers.

Mara burst into Beth's house, so out of breath she couldn't speak. Beth motioned for Mara to lay Ikee on the bed.

'Protect my baby,' Mara whispered to the heavens, something she hadn't done in a long time. 'I'll do anything. Please, just let him be well.'

Ikee stopped breathing a few hours later.

Mara emptied her stomach on the step outside as her world grew dark. She fell to the ground and gave way to the darkness.

She woke to Beth holding a cloth to her forehead. Mara groaned and lifted herself off the floor.

She looked to the bed where Ikee lay, and heard wailing from far above the room. But the sound came from her own lips. Mara lay beside him, cradling his tiny body close to hers, willing him to wake up, willing the warmth to remain.

But Ikee lay still.

She would never know joy again, never hear Ikee's voice again, never hold Levi's son again. Her baby was gone.

Day Three

Mara sat alone in Beth's room. She hadn't left since Ikee died. Her heart was a heavy stone in her chest.

Visitors streamed in to bid her child farewell. Mara barely looked up.

Old Paddy had been by. He'd sat with Mara, holding her hand. His presence was calming. She'd have liked him to stay but simply thanked him for coming when he stood to leave.

The town of Nain gathered around Mara, and she hid beneath her dark cloak. She held one hand on Ikee's small coffin as they walked towards the village gate. Today they would bury her child.

She couldn't think of his tiny face or his beautiful smile.

Ikee was her heart. When they lowered him into the ground today, her only comfort was that she would one day join him.

'Why my baby, God?' The question repeated itself.

The funeral procession moved quietly through the streets of Nain. A hand would touch her shoulder, but Mara didn't look up. She concentrated on the dirt road ahead of her shoes. It was all she could do.

She dreaded what lay ahead with a dread so thick she could taste it. The urge came to vomit, so she slowed to steady herself. Those around her slowed with her, and she felt an arm nestle under her own. She recognised Paddy's shoes and accepted the support.

As the funeral procession walked out the village gates, Mara heard a noise. She glanced up from beneath her dark shawl, and saw a crowd approaching, following a man.

Her eyes were covered and the crowd was far off, but she was drawn to the man's eyes. Her steps slowed to a stop, and she stood and watched him.

The coffin bearers stopped too. The whole procession came to a standstill.

Mara held her breath. Who was he? Why was she unable to look away from him? And was it possible that he could see her inside of her hiding place? He was fast approaching and his eyes did not leave hers.

The man seemed familiar, but Mara was sure she didn't know him. He took large strides, covering the distance between them. The crowd hushed, all eyes on their leader.

As he drew closer, Mara was overwhelmed by the look in his eyes. As though her hands had a mind of their own, she pulled the veil from her face.

Who was this man? Why did she get the feeling that he knew her?

He stopped and stood before her now. Mara's tears spilled over. Her hand dropped from Ikee's coffin to her side.

His eyes were kind and hers spoke to his without using words.

'This is my child, my baby.' Her head fell and she held her face in her hands.

'Don't cry,' he said, and she lifted her face to see him step towards Ikee's coffin.

What was he doing? She would have stopped him, but his eyes calmed her. They were filled with compassion.

He looked at her child. The bearers lowered the coffin, and Mara groaned at the sight of his small body.

The man looked back at Mara and, with dancing eyes, he reached out a hand and touched the coffin.

He turned to Ikee and leaned down towards him.

'I tell you, get up.'

Mara froze. Time stood still, and all was silent.

She held her breath and something changed inside Mara, an awareness that her life had somehow been in preparation for this moment.

Ikee's small hand moved from his chest to his face, and a gasp spread through the crowd. Fear and wonder filled the air as Ikee sat up. He looked at the man and rested his head to one side.

'Hello there,' the man said softly.

'Hello.' Ikee rubbed his eyes with both hands. 'Do you have an apple?'

The man laughed, and the baffled crowd joined him.

He lifted Ikee and placed him tenderly in Mara's arms. Tears ran down her cheeks and she kissed his little face.

Soon afterward Jesus went with his disciples to the village of Nain, and a large crowd followed him. A funeral procession was coming out as he approached the village gate.

The young man who had died was a widow's only son, and a large crowd from the village was with her. When the Lord saw her, his heart overflowed with compassion. "Don't cry!" he said. Then he walked over to the coffin and touched it, and the bearers stopped. "Young man," he said, "I tell you, get up." Then the dead boy sat up and began to talk! And Jesus gave him back to his mother. (Luke 7:11-15)

Human

Jesus was a real man, alive like you and me.
He had a life, a name, and a face.
He had foods he liked and others he did not.
He had a space bubble, a preference about whether he liked
to touch people or to greet them from a distance.
He had a smile. Sometimes he thought things were funny
and laughed out loud. Other times, tears fell down his face
with no one there to see them.
There were times when he lay on his bed, staring at his
bedroom wall, thinking his own thoughts and dreaming his
own dreams.
Jesus had hands. He would sit outside on his front step at
night, staring down at them.
He watched the moon, the same moon we see.
He cut his fingernails.
There were places he loved to go, places with familiar sights
and sounds and smells.
He had a life, like you and me, and he left it behind.
He gave it up to save us.

You must have the same attitude that Christ Jesus had.
Though he was God, he did not think of equality with
God as something to cling to.
Instead, he gave up his divine privileges; he took the

humble position of a slave and was born as a human being.

When he appeared in human form, he humbled himself in obedience to God and died a criminal's death on a cross. (Philippians 2:5-8)

Judas

He had done it. Fear and guilt sat heavily in the pit of his stomach. His mind was dark, and the voices were getting louder with each footstep. He picked up his pace and ran towards the temple, clutching the pouch in his hand. Maybe there was still time. Maybe he could still make it right. It wasn't like they'd actually harm Jesus. They couldn't. He hadn't committed a crime. He'd only spoken to the people. Spoken to them, and healed all their diseases.

Judas closed his eyes and held his fingers to the side of his head. He couldn't think straight. It had all seemed so clear at the time. Just yesterday, it had made sense. Now he could see he'd made a mistake. Like waking from a bad dream, he could see that he'd been misled. They had to understand. They'd let him make it right.

He took the temple stairs two at a time and pulled back the heavy door. It was a simple mistake. He would set things straight. Once he'd explained, it would all be sorted. No harm done.

He heard voices up ahead and knew they were there; meeting, no doubt, to discuss their successful arrest. Their voices lowered as his footsteps approached. The elders and the leading priests were huddled together, deep in hushed conversation. They barely glanced up as Judas entered.

Judas' heart beat heavily against his chest. He cleared his throat, attempting to get their attention. Just the day before, he had been their number one priority. But it was evident he was no longer of interest to them. They had needed him for one thing alone.

'Excuse me.' He approached the huddled group, determined to speak with them.

Annas, the leading priest, glanced up at Judas. Judas took the pouch from his coat and held it in front of the elderly man's face. Annas glared at the pouch, clearly annoyed at the interruption. He squinted his eyes and turned up his nose. 'What's this?'

The men stopped their murmuring and looked at Judas now. He had their full attention.

'I don't want this anymore.' His voice was hollow and shaking. 'I have sinned. I have betrayed an innocent man.' The truth in his words cut to the core of his being. What had he done? Vomit rose up in the back of his throat.

The men were unfazed. Amused. They laughed among themselves, but Annas never broke eye contact with Judas. The priest smiled a smile that didn't reach his eyes. Then he slowly shook his head from side to side.

'What do we care?' He pointed at the pouch. 'That's your problem now, isn't it Judas?'

Now Judas got it. He understood. Fear swept over him, and panic threatened to choke him. He couldn't reverse this. He couldn't make them understand, because they planned to kill Jesus.

The men laughed at Judas, their mocking voices colliding with those already screaming in his head. Judas looked from Annas to the money pouch. He lifted it high above his head and threw it down hard against the marble floor between them. The men grew silent as the pouch exploded at their feet and silver coins scattered across the floor.

Judas ran from the room and didn't stop running. The voices in his head were shrieking at him and he had to escape them. He ran fast, tears flying from his cheeks as he passed people on the road. They stopped to watch as he ran by, no doubt wondering why he was in such a rush.

He ran until his lungs felt close to exploding and he couldn't run anymore. He collapsed, out of breath, against a road sign. He was alone now on the deserted road. He sat heavily on the gravel, resting his head between his knees and struggled to catch his breath. What had he done? How could he live with this? Would they really kill Jesus? Judas knew the answer to that question. He had seen it in the priest's eyes.

He wiped the tears from his face. There was a large piece of rope on the road beside him. It was grey and dirty but had probably been white once upon a time. Judas eyeballed it for a minute before reaching for it. He wrapped it around his hand a couple of times, tugging it hard with the other.

He stood and steadied himself on the road sign he'd been leaning against. There was something written there. He used the rope around his hand to wipe away the cobwebs covering the sign's message.

The Potter's Field. Enquiries within.

When Judas, who had betrayed him, realised that Jesus had been condemned to die, he was filled with remorse. So he took the thirty pieces of silver back to the leading priests and the elders. 'I have sinned,' he declared, 'for I have betrayed an innocent man.'

'What do we care?' they retorted. 'That's your problem.'

Then Judas threw the silver coins down in the Temple and went out and hanged himself. (Matthew 27:3-5)

Zebina's Cushion

The musty old cushion had once been rich blue, but it was faded now. It had seen better days and held many heads over the years. It was handmade by a woman named Zebina, who made clothing for a living. She had spun, woven and dyed a large piece of linen to make an outfit for her son. When it was completed, there was fabric left over, so she made a cushion.

Zebina had gifted the brilliant blue tunic and cushion to her son. He'd placed the cushion in his sleeping room and his children had taken turns with it. Sometimes it was used as a weapon when the younger children bounced around together. Other times, it held their heads as they slept.

The blue linen cushion was taken by the family to a wedding one night. They would be up late into the evening and the youngest might need to sleep. But when they arrived, she'd dropped it on a chair and got busy playing with her friends. The cushion had remained there long after her family left.

It spent many years in the guest room of its new home, where the sun shone directly onto it, day after day, and faded its brilliant blue to a muted sky colour.

When the cushion was placed on a stool in the courtyard one day, a visiting traveller sat on it as he ate. Then, as he prepared to leave, the cushion was gifted to him, along with a warm blanket for his journey ahead.

The cushion was taken from place to place and saw more

bed mats and nights under the stars than it could count. One day, the traveller with the blue cushion boarded a boat. He just needed a ride to the other side of the lake. On arriving and thanking the boat owner, he jumped ashore without taking the cushion. He'd long gone by the time the boat owner found it, so it remained there, swaying back and forth on the lake. The cushion sat on a bench seat at the back of the boat and was leaned on, sat on, and slept on by many fishermen.

One day, a Jewish rabbi laid his head on the blue linen cushion. He breathed deeply of its musky scent and his face felt the stories it held against his cheek. He turned his head to face the inside of the boat, his eyes close to the wooden side, his disciples behind him. He closed his eyes and listened to them talking among themselves. He smiled to himself as he listened to their conversation. Stretching out his legs, he wrapped both arms around the cushion beneath his head, and let the gentle rocking of the boat sway him to and fro until he slept.

Suddenly the cushion was shaken beneath his head and he opened his eyes.

'Teacher!' A disciple stood above him, his eyes full of fear. 'Don't you care that we're going to drown?'

Jesus lifted his head from the blue cushion and stood. The boat rocked violently back and forth. With nothing holding it still, the cushion was thrown from its bench seat. It fell to the floor of the boat where water soaked into it.

Jesus held the side of the boat for balance as he looked out at the raging waters.

'Silence! Be still!' he called out.

The wind stopped instantly. The waves ceased, the boat stood still, and all was calm. The blue cushion was wet right the way through.

Jesus turned to his disciples and looked at them without saying a word. There was silence aboard the boat as the disciples stood, stunned.

'Why are you afraid? Do you still have no faith?' He finally asked them.

The disciples moved to tidy up the boat, retrieving all that had been thrown around, including the blue cushion. It was placed back on a bench seat to dry out.

'Who is this man?' Simon whispered to the other disciples. 'Even the wind and waves obey him!'

But soon a fierce storm came up. High waves were breaking into the boat, and it began to fill with water.

Jesus was sleeping at the back of the boat with his head on a cushion. The disciples woke him up, shouting, 'Teacher, don't you care that we're going to drown?'

When Jesus woke up, he rebuked the wind and said to the waves, 'Silence! Be still!' Suddenly the wind stopped, and there was a great calm. Then he asked them, 'Why are you afraid? Do you still have no faith?'

The disciples were absolutely terrified. 'Who is this man?' they asked each other. 'Even the wind and waves obey him!' (Mark 4:37-41)

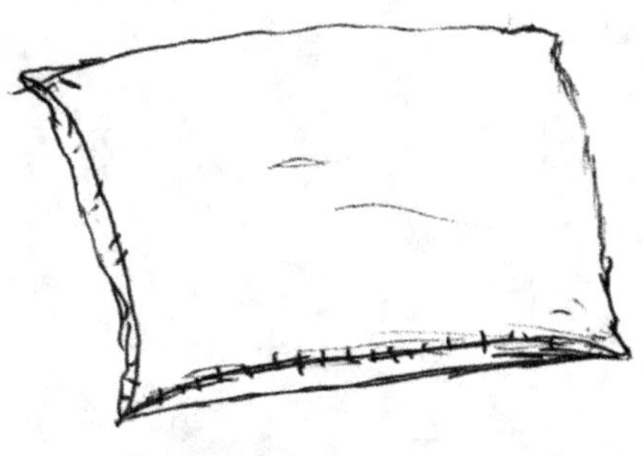

There's a hole in my heart
that's shaped like your place of rest.

Oh God, you are my God; I earnestly search for you.
My soul thirsts for you; my whole body longs for you…
(Psalm 63:1)

Buz

'Daddy!' Lilli called out to Buz. She reached her arms high; Buz lifted her and held her close. She wrapped her arms around his neck and he kissed her closed eyelids. Lilli giggled and moved her thumbs around to his face, smoothing out his eyebrows.

'I'm straightening your caterpillars, Daddy,' she whispered to him. He smiled, cherishing the warmth of her breath against his face and the touch of her fingers against his skin.

It wasn't real. She wasn't there. He sensed her leaving, slipping away before she'd faded. Buz tried to hold on to her, wrestling with consciousness, until his arms were empty.

She was gone. He felt the rock, a hard pillow beneath his head. He lay still and held on to her memory while it was close, willing the sound of her voice to stay near.

He opened his eyes. His head lay close to the carvings of a tombstone. He knew the words without reading them. He knew the inscriptions well, not just on this tomb, but on all of them.

His head pounded, and dried blood spread across his face. He licked his parched lips and could taste its distinctive flavour.

He'd raged through the night, and his throat was raw from howling. He was always aware of where he was and what he was doing, but he no longer belonged to himself.

Memories of his girls he'd left behind, led him to cut himself with sharp rocks in the hills. His arms were lined with scars both old and new. One of these days, one of these cuts could be his last.

They had tried to contain him again a few days earlier. The townspeople of the Gerasenes were afraid of him. They didn't feel safe visiting those resting in the burial caves.

But Buz's strength wasn't his own. He simply snapped the chains from his wrist and smashed the shackles holding him. He was as surprised as those guarding him at the power of his strength. They could never contain him.

Sometimes he wished they could.

He dreamt of them often, Lilli and Hannah. He remembered a time when they weren't afraid of him. A time when he knew the creases in their delicate hands as though they were his own. There was a time when he couldn't imagine being away from them. They would be older now. They would be afraid of him.

He didn't understand what had happened. But he knew something had taken him over. There were others now who controlled his mind. He knew their voices well. Buz doubted he would live to see his girls again. His life was lost to him.

Buz lifted his head now from the concrete and pulled himself up. He could hear the pigs feeding on the hillside beside the graveyard. His head hurt, and he needed water.

He stumbled down to the water's edge and dropped to his knees. He used his blood-stained hands to cup the water to his mouth. The lake was so clear today that he could see the stones beneath shining where the sunlight hit the water. His mind was calm, but he knew it wouldn't last long. It never did.

Suddenly he heard something unusual. Voices. And they weren't inside his head! He sat upright, crouching like a wild animal and scanned his surroundings. It was a boat! A boat on the lake, and it seemed to be heading for shore.

Buz kept low and moved fast, back up towards the cemetery. He crouched beside a burial cave and watched from his hiding place.

The travellers were laughing. They obviously weren't from these parts, or they would have known better than to come near his graveyard.

The voices inside Buz's head returned, whispering as though waking up from sleep. They hissed and snarled, growing louder and louder until their shrieking was all Buz could hear. It echoed and rang through his ears.

But there was something different. Today, the voices tormenting him were in a panic.

There was chaos inside his head, more than usual. He couldn't keep up with what they were saying. He didn't understand what they were screaming. He dug his fingernails into the top of his head, ripping through his flesh. He pulled his fingers down over his face, reopening old wounds.

He howled, unable to contain the noise in his mind. He howled over and over, trying to drown out the screaming voices in his head.

The passengers aboard the boat were silent now. They must have heard his howling. Buz watched their worried faces as they looked up towards the burial caves. As the boat met the shore, they jumped from it one at a time. They looked cautious and remained on the shore. A man in a long white robe stepped from the boat. The others watched him, looking to him for direction.

The man turned without hesitation and walked straight towards the burial caves. Straight towards where Buz was hiding.

Buz watched the man's face from where he knelt. The voices so loud now, he couldn't stand it. They were out of control. He had to do something.

Buz leapt out from where he was crouching, out into the open, in full sight of the men.

The man in the white robe stopped. He didn't seem shocked by Buz's swift appearance.

He looked Buz in the eyes, and then something new happened. A voice spoke inside Buz's head, a voice he didn't recognise. The voice was calm and clear and nothing like the others.

'Come out of the man, you evil spirit,' the voice said. There was an authority in this voice, one that made Buz stop in his tracks.

His head reeled, and the other voices became louder and louder. The man was still quite a way off and Buz ran the distance between them and was thrown to the ground before him. He bowed low, with his face to the stones. He had no control over his body.

'Why are you interfering with me, Jesus, Son of the Most High God?' he shrieked. The words were new to Buz. Who did the voices speak of? 'In the name of God, I beg you, don't torture me.'

The man they called Jesus knelt before Buz and looked him in the eyes.

'What is your name?' It was clear he wasn't speaking to Buz.

'My name is Legion, because there are many of us inside this man,' the voices replied. They chorused together, one over the other, begging with Jesus not to send them to some distant place.

Buz listened and waited. Jesus looked calm; there was no fear in his eyes.

Buz lifted his head up high then and clutched the stones in his clenched fists. His head was thrown down against the stones. He didn't black out but lay before Jesus, dazed.

The voices were wild and fearful.

'Send us into those pigs,' they screamed. 'Let us enter them.' Buz remembered the pigs feeding on the hillside, but didn't understand what they meant. Was it possible the voices in his head could leave him? Could they live inside a pig instead?

Buz pulled his head back up from the stones. Jesus stood and looked out at the surrounding hills, watching the pigs.

Buz braced himself for another collision with the stones but Jesus swiftly knelt back down. His eyes were ablaze with power. He looked at Buz and with a simple nod, the voices were silenced.

A weight lifted off Buz, and he laid his head down on the stones. He closed his eyes, inhaled deeply, and wept. Jesus placed his hand on the back of Buz's head and held it there.

Jesus and his friends were leaving. As they boarded their boat, a panic came over Buz. He wanted to go with Jesus.

Buz jumped up from the rock where he sat. All eyes were on him, but he didn't care. Jesus had restored his mind and Buz needed to stay with him. He pushed past the disciples and reached out to grab Jesus by the shoulder.

Jesus turned and looked at Buz. A peace came over Buz. But words escaped him. He looked down to the rocks at their feet.

'Please let me come with you.' Buz looked back up into Jesus' eyes. 'I'll go wherever you go and I'll do whatever you do.' Buz meant every word of it.

Jesus looked into Buz's eyes, as though searching his soul. 'No,' He replied, shaking his head. 'Go home.' He spoke in a whisper. 'Go home to your family.' When Jesus said the word 'family', Buz got the feeling that Jesus thought of Buz's girls. Could he have known about Lilli and Hannah?

'And tell them everything the Lord has done for you, and how merciful he has been.' He nodded at Buz with a knowing smile, and turned to step into the boat.

Go home? Go home! He could go home. The realisation was overwhelming. He could leave this graveyard, and he could see his children again. He turned and ran through the crowd, who separated to create a path for him.

A path to run home.

So they arrived at the other side of the lake, in the region of the Gerasenes. When Jesus climbed out of the boat, a man possessed by an evil spirit came out from a cemetery to meet him. This man lived among the burial caves and could no longer be restrained, even with a chain... Day and night he wandered among the burial caves and in the hills, howling and cutting himself with sharp stones.

When Jesus was still some distance away, the man saw him, ran to meet him, and bowed low before him. With a shriek, he screamed, 'Why are you interfering with me, Jesus, Son of the Most High God? In the name of God, I beg you, don't torture me!' For Jesus had already said to the spirit, 'Come out of the man, you evil spirit.'

Then Jesus demanded, 'What is your name?'

And he replied, 'My name is Legion, because there are many of us inside this man...'

'Send us into those pigs,' the spirits begged. 'Let us enter them.'

So Jesus gave them permission. The evil spirits came out of the man and entered the pigs…

A crowd soon gathered around Jesus, and they saw the man who had been freed from the demons. He was sitting at Jesus' feet, fully clothed and perfectly sane, and they were all afraid.

As Jesus was getting into the boat, the man who had been demon possessed begged to go with him. But Jesus said, 'No, go home to your family, and tell them every-thing the Lord has done for you and how merciful he has been.' (Mark 5:1-3, 5-9, 12-13, 18-19; Luke 8:35)

Susie

Susie sat outside in front of the fire, warming her hands before her. It was late and dark, and she was the only one still awake. Susie looked around. How her life had changed in the past couple of months. It was extraordinary.

Susie had grown up in a privileged home. She had never felt the pangs of hunger or been in need of anything. Her parents had showered her with gifts from an early age, the finest of everything and then handpicked a rich husband for her. Susie had married Gene at seventeen, and it had been an agreeable union. They'd had several happy years together, and their wealth had increased.

Although Susie had every good thing that money could buy, she'd often found herself with an emptiness inside, an emptiness she didn't understand. The emptiness had grown throughout the years, and she could never satisfy it, no matter how hard she tried. Beautiful dresses, fancy parties, brand new homes, and delicious delicacies. Nothing filled the gap that ached to be filled.

Gene fell ill and died shortly afterwards, and Susie had missed him terribly. She'd had a ridiculous amount of money to her name, so much wealth that she hardly knew what to do with it. But she was empty, empty and alone. The emptiness had grown when Gene died. Or perhaps Susie's awareness had grown, now she no longer had the distraction of constant company. She was left alone with her thoughts and had found herself face-to-face with some big questions. Why was she here? What was her purpose? Would she ever find something to fill her ever-growing void?

But then she met Jesus and everything about her life changed.

She held her hands back up to warm them in front of the fire. She hardly recognised them – her once perfectly manicured fingernails were dirty and rough. These were hands that knew how to light a fire and cook outdoors under a blanket of stars. Hands that had helped to set up bed mats beneath the moon for herself and the entire team she now travelled with to different villages. Hands that daily wiped tears from her cheeks as she sat before the teacher and listened while he spoke to the crowds.

She was no longer perfectly put together and living in luxury, but she had never felt full the way she did now, never been alive the way she was now.

When Susie had first heard Jesus speak all those months back, his words had touched the emptiness inside her. Since that day, his words had slowly but surely, little by little, filled the space inside.

Susie had found a meaning for her extraordinary wealth. She had never enjoyed spending money on herself the way she enjoyed funding this venture. Without a doubt, camping beneath the stars with Jesus and his team was the most fulfilling time of Susie's life.

She stood up from where she sat beside the fire. Everyone was fast asleep, and Susie should head to bed as well. She was exhausted but deeply satisfied.

There was a shuffle at the tent door, and Jesus stepped out into the moonlight. He spotted Susie and smiled at her. She loved him, but not in the way she had loved her father or Gene. She enjoyed serving Jesus, preparing his food and taking care of his needs. Susie knew his routines well and loved everything about travelling with him and the rest of the group – the food, the tents, the inside jokes, the laughter around the campfire each night. It was special.

'Good night, Susie,' Jesus whispered.

'Good night,' she replied.

Jesus quietly walked away from the camp and into the trees lining their campground. Jesus often left in the night. Susie knew this because she was always the last to go to sleep. He gave so much of himself away during his days and would refuel by praying the night away.

Susie watched him until he was out of sight, then she crept to her bed mat beside her friends, her new family. As she lay in bed, she thought of how Jesus' words had filled the empty space within her. In fact, it wasn't only full. It was bubbling over. Susie had a deep sense of peace as she fell asleep.

Soon afterward Jesus began a tour of the nearby towns and villages, preaching and announcing the Good News about the Kingdom of God. He took his twelve disciples with him, along with some women he had healed and from whom he had cast out evil spirits. Among them were Mary Magdalene, from whom he had cast out seven demons; Joanna, the wife of Chuza, Herod's business manager; Susanna; and many others who were contributing from their own resources to support Jesus and his disciples. (Luke 8:1-3)

Sons of Thunder

They were hard to contain and impossible to control.

Most fishermen were rough sorts, but the brothers were roughest of all. Some called them hot-headed and easily angered. But when it came to those close to them, the brothers were incredibly loyal and staunchly devoted.

Their father went grey prematurely and nobody blamed him. His sons often fought with each other. But when threatened by outsiders, they were a tight unit, a force to be reckoned with.

It was late at night, and dark. A small light lit up the corner of the room, the only light that could be seen.

A storm was brewing outside, so the brothers had the night off. But they were restless – their bodies told them it was time to work while others were sleeping.

They bickered and fought with one another before lying down on the floor for an arm wrestle. It was a good way to let off steam. They thrived on the competition.

They were evenly matched in strength and the arm wrestle went on and on. When James hit his brother's hand to the ground, loud thunder roared from outside the door, the clouds came crashing together high up above them.

Afterward Jesus went up on a mountain and called out the ones he wanted to go with him. And they came to him.

James and John (the sons of Zebedee, but Jesus nicknamed them 'Sons of Thunder')... (Mark 3:13, 17)

Milo

Milo pulled his sheepskin coat over his shoulders. The temperature had dropped when night fell. The sheep in his fold were scattered about, grazing peacefully. Milo stretched his head back to a vista of stars. He loved nights like this, with the beauty of creation at his fingertips.

In the whispering of the night sky, he sometimes felt as if someone called his name from the stillness. He was pulled from his thoughts by the rustle of leather pouches. It was time to eat, and he was hungry.

Picking up his rod from the grass at his feet, he walked the short distance to his friends. They nestled down on a flat clearing of thick grass. They would sleep well tonight, taking turns to watch over their flocks.

'What's for dinner?' Milo winked at Art. Everyone knew Art was not one for sharing his food. Art laughed

'Always a trier, Milo. I'll give you that.' Art's wife, Shelah, was an incredible cook. She packed him delicacies most shepherds could only dream of. But Art was a beast of a man and always hungry. Milo liked to play with him.

'I spoke to Shelah and told her how much I love her stuffed olives, so she packed an extra portion for me in your pouch.' Milo had Art's full attention.

Obi stifled a grin and Milo laughed at the look of concern on Art's face. Art grunted and pulled out his olives.

'I'd chuck these at you if they weren't so good.' Milo

pulled out some bread and cheese. He'd packed it himself. He admired what Art had with Shelah. But Milo was devoted only to his sheep.

Milo scanned his fold back and forth until he found Gracie. She was the smallest and he felt especially protective of her.

'Gracie!' Milo called. She followed his voice until she was close enough to touch.

'Here you go, girl.' He offered his last bite.

'You know they all can tell Milo?' Obi asked.

'They can't.' Milo laughed. Great. Now it was his turn to cop some slack.

'They definitely can,' Art said.

He pointed out over the flock.

'When's the last time you shared your bread with old Edna, or Phily over there?'

'Let's call them over for a stuffed olive if you're so concerned about their feelings.' Milo grinned.

The hours rolled by comfortably, and chitchat between friends became yawning and setting up sleep stations.

As Milo rolled out his mat, he heard an unusual sound. He stopped short. His friends froze as well. Milo scanned the fold. Was it a hyena … or a lion?

A minute passed, and the men were silent and still.

'Has it gone?' Obi finally whispered.

'No.' The voice was loud and clear … but the voice didn't belong to them.

Milo spun around, looking to the left and the right. A man stood before them, who appeared from nowhere. Light surrounded him and his body shone like fire.

Milo fell to his knees. Obi and Art followed. Then he froze, too frightened to speak.

The light encasing the man crept towards them until it fell over where they knelt. Milo trembled from head to toe. What was happening? Who was this man?

'Don't be afraid.' The stranger's voice was strong. Milo looked from the grass into his eyes. The man nodded, and Milo swallowed over the lump in his throat and the thump-thump-thump of his heartbeat ringing in his ears. It was the only sound against the silence of the night.

'I bring you good news that will bring great joy to all people,' the stranger said. 'The Saviour – yes, the Messiah, the Lord has been born today in Bethlehem, the city of David!'

Milo held his breath, transfixed, as the man spoke. Milo hung on his every word as though his life depended on them.

'You will recognise him by this sign,' the being continued. 'You will find a baby wrapped snugly in strips of cloth, lying in a manger.'

Suddenly the man wasn't alone but was joined by others. A whole army of angels filled the sky.

'Glory to God in highest heaven, peace on earth to those with whom God is pleased,' they called out, their voices rising together like a beautiful, terrifying song.

And then there was silence, the night sky was as it had been – empty. Speechless, Milo looked to his friends. Milo laughed and cried. Obi and Art joined him.

'We have to go to Bethlehem,' Milo finally said. 'We have to search for the baby, the newborn Saviour.'

That night there were shepherds staying in the fields nearby, guarding their flocks of sheep. Suddenly, an angel of the Lord appeared among them, and the radiance of the Lord's glory surrounded them. They were terrified, but the angel reassured them. 'Don't be afraid!' he said. 'I bring you good news that will bring great joy to all people. The Saviour – yes, the Messiah, the Lord – has been born today in Bethlehem, the city of David! And you will recognise him by this sign: You will find a baby wrapped snugly in strips of cloth, lying in a manger.'

Suddenly, the angel was joined by a vast host of others – the armies of heaven – praising God and saying, 'Glory to God in highest heaven, and peace on earth to those with whom God is pleased.' (Luke 2:8-14)

A Chosen Stone

A stone lay on the floor of a streambed. The stone had sat in the stream for many years. Sometimes when the rain fell hard, the stone would shift a little this way or that. But it never went far. The sunlight often found the stone, bringing it to light for a few hours each day. Other times, the stone sat in the shadow of a tree that grew beside the stream.

Today the sun shone bright and the stream was calm. The stone sat on the floor of the stream as it always had. A boy stood above the stream, peering down into the water. He was young and handsome with dark features. He looked at the stones for a minute or two before he reached beneath the surface, wrapped his fingers around the stone, and pulled it from its resting place.

The stone had been chosen and was placed into the boy's shepherd bag. It sat in the dark and the water from its smooth surface soaked into the fabric.

The stone was taken from the bag and placed into a sling. The sling was pulled back, and the stone was hurled through the air. It travelled fast and hit the forehead of a giant. The stone sank into the flesh of his forehead. The large man fell face down on the ground before the shepherd boy.

He picked up five smooth stones from a stream and put them into his shepherd's bag. Then, armed only with his shepherd's staff and sling, he started across the valley to fight the Philistine.

As Goliath moved closer to attack, David quickly ran out to meet him. Reaching into his shepherd's bag and taking out a stone, he hurled it with his sling and hit the Philistine in the forehead. The stone sank in, and Goliath stumbled and fell face down on the ground. (1 Samuel 17:40, 48-49)

Hail

Hail huddled around the fire with her family. They shared the lamb with their neighbours, the Tailors. There would have been too much for the four of them – Hail, her younger brother Micah, and her parents.

Those had been the instructions. The whole animal must be eaten or burnt. Hail was nervous and struggling to eat her share. She leaned back and glanced down the road. There were campfires as far down as the Haras' place on the corner. Every street would look the same in the Israelite neighbourhoods tonight. They would be careful to do everything the right way. She could barely believe it was happening.

It was hard to imagine anything would come of it. Was it possible for life to be different from the way it had always been? Was 'freedom' ever attainable for her people?

She'd watched the Egyptians her entire life, in awe of their freedom. She never dared to believe that she, a young Israelite girl, a slave of Egypt, could ever be free.

That was until Moses had returned to Egypt. He'd brought with him hope for her people. Hail had been fascinated at the stories told around the campfires. Stories of Moses going to Pharaoh himself and commanding him, 'God said to let his people go.'

Then she had seen the plagues with her own eyes. The frogs and the gnats. The water had turned to blood. The plagues hadn't touched the Israelite community. But they had drowned the Egyptians homes, covered their skin with boils, and taken Hail's breath away.

God was doing something. He was moving, and she could see it with her own eyes. For the first time in her life, in her parents' and her grandparents' lives, something was happening.

And tonight was the night. Hail had been out earlier, collecting hyssop branches with Micah. He didn't understand the significance of their meaning. Hail was fourteen, though, and she understood. Her heart had pounded hard inside her chest whenever she thought about the possibilities of the night ahead.

Hail's father had dipped the branches into the blood of the lamb and let Hail climb up to paint their doorpost red. He'd dipped it several more times to paint down the sides of the door frame. They must be sure it was done properly.

Hail looked down at the meat in her hand, then up at her mother's face flickering in the firelight.

'Eat up, Hail. You need your energy.' Her mother was nervous – Hail could see it in her eyes. But there was something else, an expression Hail barely recognised. Her mother was excited. There had been little to feel excited about in her mother's life.

The butterflies in Hail's stomach flip-flopped when she thought of the prospect of change for her parents. The lines in her mother's face were too deep for the number of years she had lived.

'Please help us, God.' Hail whispered the silent prayer, a prayer unanswered until now.

They were all fully dressed. Hail had helped Micah with his sandals before putting on her own. He'd looked at her, surprised. It was night-time, and he was usually putting his sleeping clothes on. But not tonight. Those had been the instructions. 'Wear your sandals, be fully dressed, eat with urgency.'

Hail's stomach turned. How could she eat when something big was about to happen? And something was. She could feel it in the excitement buzzing in the air, in the hushed preparations and nervous whispers. What would it be? What would he do?

Surely there was no way they could escape from Egypt. There were so many people! Pharaoh would never let them leave. Whatever way she looked at it, Hail couldn't figure it out. It seemed impossible.

They finished eating, and Hail's father burnt the remainder of their lamb. They kissed the Tailor family goodnight and went indoors. It was a calm, clear night, and the moon shone bright. Hard to imagine that anything out of the ordinary would happen on a night like tonight.

Hail stood on the step, examining the dried blood, then took a deep breath and walked inside. Her father fastened the bar, locking the door behind them.

Hail sighed. 'Can you guys believe this is happening? I can hardly think straight.'

Micah looked up from where he'd plonked himself on the floor. 'What's happening?' he asked.

'We're asking ourselves that same question, Micah.' Hail smiled. 'Are you ready for a bedtime story?'

They lay together on Micah's bed, fully dressed and wearing their sandals. Hail told him one story after another until he slept. Hail sat down beside her parents.

'Will you sleep tonight?' Hail asked.

Her father shook his head. 'We'll wait up a while.'

'Me too.' Hail nodded. 'I couldn't sleep if I tried!'

The hours passed slowly. Hail paced the room back and forth, before sitting down again next to her dozing parents. Their heads rested on one another, and her father snored. She smiled at them before shifting restlessly, then jumped back up to resume her pacing.

It was just on midnight when she heard something. She froze mid-step in the middle of the room.

An unusual sound came from just outside the door, like the howling of wind but on the stillest of nights. It seemed out of place as it rushed by the door. Just like that, the sound was gone.

Hail let out her breath and fixed her eyes on the door. Could that sound have been something? Could that have been him? Her parents hadn't even stirred.

She sat down and leaned against the front door. Maybe she should peek her head out the door … just in case something had happened. But that was dangerous. She'd have to wait.

She pulled up her knees and rested her head on her arms, feeling sleepy all of a sudden.

Hail woke up with a fright, and wiped the drool from her cheek. What had woken her?

The oddest of sounds. She sat still and listened.

There it was again, the sound of wailing. The sound of many voices joining together in the same sad song. She jumped to her feet as the sound grew louder.

'Mum, Dad, something's happening.' They opened their eyes as Hail reached for the front door.

She poked her head outside. It was dark and cool. Her eyes adjusted to the darkness and she could see others coming out from their homes. She flung the door open. The wailing was so loud it filled the air, a heart-rending, frightening sound.

What could it be? What had happened? What had he done?

'Announce to the whole community of Israel that on the tenth day of this month each family must choose a lamb or a young goat for a sacrifice, one animal for each household. If a family is too small to eat a whole animal, let them share with another family in the neighbourhood...

'Then the whole assembly of the community of Israel must slaughter their lamb or young goat at twilight. They are to take some of the blood and smear it on the sides and top of the doorframes of the houses where they eat the animal. That same night they must roast the meat over a fire and eat it...

'These are your instructions for eating this meal: Be fully dressed, wear your sandals, and carry your walking stick in your hand. Eat the meal with urgency, for this is the Lord's Passover.'

And that night at midnight, the Lord struck down all the firstborn sons in the land of Egypt, from the firstborn son of Pharaoh, who sat on his throne, to the firstborn son of the prisoner in the dungeon. Even the firstborn of their livestock were killed. Pharaoh and all his officials and all the people of Egypt woke up during the night, and loud wailing was heard throughout the land of Egypt. There was not a single house where someone had not died.
(Exodus 12:3-4, 6-8, 11, 29-30)

Salo

Salo was a sparrow who loved to fly. But she hadn't eaten for days. She could feel her energy dropping as she soared with her flock.

She needed food, and fast. They all did. Salo hadn't gone this long without eating before.

She kept her eyes on the ground, in search of food, in search of anything she could find. But there was nothing.

Where were they? Why had they come here? And what would happen if she didn't eat soon?

Hours passed by, and Salo wasn't doing well. It wasn't long before she felt light-headed and consciousness began to slip away.

She struggled to stay awake, struggled to stay airborne, but starvation had taken its toll.

Salo fell.

She fell and fell and fell until she hit the ground with a thud and was no longer.

He knew.

He lifted his head from where he sat, and he looked up from what he was doing.

He saw her descent, and he knew that she fell.

Salo was caught on the other side of life. She found herself flying through a golden sky.

No longer hungry and no longer distressed, but full of peace.

*What is the price of two sparrows – one copper coin? But
not a single sparrow can fall to the ground without your
Father knowing it. And the very hairs on your head are
all numbered. So don't be afraid; you are more valuable to
God than a whole flock of sparrows.* (Matthew 10:29-31)

Saul

He hated them. As far as Saul was concerned, they were ruining everything. He refused to sit still and watch.

He had plans to put this madness to an end. All this talk about Jesus being the Messiah. He'd even heard some calling him God's own son. It made him sick.

Saul had witnessed people being killed after admitting to their belief in Jesus. He was looking forward to seeing more of the same.

There was one God and God certainly did not have a son.

Saul visited the high priest and requested letters for the synagogues in Damascus. The letters asked for their cooperation in the arrest of any Jesus followers. Men or women, he didn't care. He just wanted to see them in chains.

Saul gathered his most trustworthy friends to help him carry out his plan in Damascus. The four of them set off by foot for the long journey.

They spent their days discussing their shared hatred of the Jesus followers.

'I don't understand why anyone would continue to believe in a dead man,' Archie said.

'It makes no sense,' Saul agreed.

'The man's dead!' Archie said. 'Wouldn't that be proof enough for his followers that Jesus wasn't who he claimed to be?'

They all nodded, stepping one foot in front of another, travelling the dusty road to Damascus.

The following morning, Saul woke before daybreak. He felt the familiar seething in his spirit before he'd even opened his eyes. He gazed up into the night sky and pondered why he felt so angry. Some mornings his anger worried him, even shocked him, although he would never admit it. His hatred towards the Jesus followers was unlike anything he'd felt before.

He knew what he was doing was right. Those following Jesus had betrayed God. But what Saul didn't understand was why the anger took over his mind and soul every waking second. It consumed his days and haunted his nights.

He always arrived back at the same conclusion – he was so passionate about obeying God. Saul would do anything to protect the truth about God. He wouldn't stop until all those following Jesus were ruined.

Saul and his friends would arrive in Damascus today. His heart leapt at the thought of carrying out his mission. Once his friends had woken, they prepared quickly and walked fast. After a few hours, they could see the faint outline of Damascus in the distance.

'We've made it!' Saul let out a cheer, encouraging laughter from his friends. He held the letters protectively in his pouch. He planned to deliver them today. The Jesus followers wouldn't know what had hit them.

They stopped for a drink of water and then set off again. All of a sudden, a light as bright as the sun shone down around Saul. He fell to the ground, blinded. His hands and his knees hit hard, and he closed his eyes to shield them from the light. He heard his friends cry out, but couldn't see them. He couldn't see anything.

'Saul, Saul! Why are you persecuting me?' a voice Saul didn't recognise spoke. Saul shook, more afraid than he'd ever been.

'Who are you, Lord?' he asked.

'I am Jesus, the one you are persecuting!' Saul held his arms over his head, stunned and speechless.

'Now, get up and go into the city, and you will be told what you must do.'

Saul stumbled around. He could tell the light had disappeared, but he could no longer see. When he opened his eyes, he saw only darkness.

Saul's friends were shocked and silent. They clasped Saul's hands and led him into the city of Damascus.

Saul's life was transformed that day. Jesus changed Saul's name to Paul and set his heart on fire with a new mission.

Saul was imprisoned for speaking about his belief in Jesus. In prison, he wrote letters to the churches he had founded.

His letters make up a big part of the New Testament of the Holy Bible.

Meanwhile, Saul was uttering threats with every breath and was eager to kill the Lord's followers. So he went to the high priest. He requested letters addressed to the synagogues in Damascus, asking for their cooperation in the arrest of any followers of the Way he found there. He wanted to bring them – both men and women – back to Jerusalem in chains.

As he was approaching Damascus on this mission, a light from heaven suddenly shone down around him. He fell to the ground and heard a voice saying to him, 'Saul! Saul! Why are you persecuting me?'

'Who are you, lord?' Saul asked.

And the voice replied, 'I am Jesus, the one you are persecuting! Now get up and go into the city, and you will be told what you must do.'

The men with Saul stood speechless, for they heard the sound of someone's voice but saw no one! Saul picked himself up off the ground, but when he opened his eyes he was blind. So his companions led him by the hand to Damascus. (Acts 9:1-8)

Ivvah

Ivvah and Koa would die now. Ivvah knew it was the truth even as she collected sticks to prepare their final meal, yet it still didn't feel real. She couldn't comprehend that tomorrow would mark the beginning of their end. By this time tomorrow evening Koa would be hungry, he'd be looking to her for food and she would have nothing left to give him.

Their starvation would begin. It would take weeks. Koa was young and fit and he would fight for his life. Ivvah knew that if she were alone, as awful as it would be, she would be alright. But she feared the thought of watching Koa starve to death. She would do anything, sacrifice anything, to save her son's life.

'Mama.' Koa poked his wee head out from inside the door. 'I'm hungry.'

'Come and help me collect sticks, and I'll cook us some dinner.' Ivvah smiled at her son, her pride and joy, trying not to imagine what she would reply to those same words the following day.

Koa jumped out the door, full of energy. He ran circles around Ivvah, collecting sticks. Ivvah prayed to God as she collected. She prayed that he would rescue her son, that he would let him live.

Koa disappeared back inside, leaving his pile of sticks outside for her. Ivvah walked back towards their home when she spotted a good-sized stick and turned back to retrieve it.

As she rose, a man stood before her. He'd appeared out of nowhere! Ivvah jumped back.

'Hello,' she said. He looked tired, as though he'd been travelling. He smiled at Ivvah.

'Would you please bring me a little water in a cup?' he asked. Water she could manage, but the famine was harsh and she had nothing else to offer him. She nodded in response and went to fetch him a cup.

'Can you bring me a bite of bread, too?' he called after her. Ivvah stopped in her tracks and turned back to the stranger. This she could not do. She must save what little she had for her son, for their last meal together.

'I swear by the Lord your God that I don't have a single piece of bread in the house.' She glanced back to her home, to make sure Koa was out of earshot. 'I have only a handful of flour left in the jar and a little cooking oil in the bottom of the jug.' She paused, and the stranger waited. 'I was just gathering a few sticks to cook this last meal. Then my son and I will die.' Her words were a whisper. She hadn't said the words out loud until now and her eyes filled with tears at the harsh reality.

Ivvah looked up from the dirt at her feet into the stranger's eyes. He was an odd man – there was something different about him.

'Don't be afraid.' He spoke with such authority and assurance that for a moment, Ivvah could almost believe he might be able to help her. But he didn't even have food or water for himself. How would this stranger help feed them if he couldn't even feed himself?

'Go ahead and do just what you've said,' he told Ivvah. 'But make a little bread for me first. Then use what's left to prepare a meal for yourself and your son. For this is what the

Lord, the God of Israel, says: There will always be flour and olive oil left in your containers until the time when the Lord sends rain and the crops grow again!'

Ivvah stood still, her mouth open. Who was this man? Could he hear from the living God? Koa poked his head out the door. He must have heard her talking.

'Mama,' he called as he came outside. 'Hello,' he said with a beaming smile. 'Would you like to come inside our house?'

Ivvah stood speechless. She didn't know what to think. Had God heard her prayers? Could she trust this man? Or was he crazy and would she share the last of their food with a stranger?

She followed Koa and the stranger inside, and got to work preparing the bread. As she worked and listened to him speak kindly to her son, a seed of hope grew in her chest. He seemed like a wise man. Perhaps he could hear from God.

Ivvah shook the flour jar until it was empty, using the last of the flour and scraping the little olive oil that was left from her jug to prepare their final meal. That was it. That was the end.

She found it hard to eat her share of the bread. Instead, she watched Koa inhale his in a matter of minutes. He was a growing boy, always hungry. The stranger smiled at her, nodding towards her meal, and she knew he was encouraging her to eat, to trust in his words, to trust in God. She was thankful he'd shown up tonight, if for no other reason than for the company and the distraction. It would have been a terrifying night to be alone. She was thankful for the glimmer of hope, even if hope was all it was.

Early the following morning, Ivvah opened her eyes well before anyone else had woken. She crept off her bed mat and into the kitchen, where she pulled her flour jar and olive oil jug off the counter. She opened them, and there was a little left in the bottom of each.

She blinked unbelieving eyes. She knew she had used the last of them the night before – she remembered shaking them completely dry. But here before her was a little flour in the bottom of the jar and a little olive oil in the bottom of the jug. She wiped the teardrop from her cheek and looked over to the bed mat where the stranger slept.

Who was this man God had sent into her home to save Koa and herself from certain death?

So he went to Zarephath. As he arrived at the gates of the village, he saw a widow gathering sticks, and he asked her, 'Would you please bring me a little water in a cup?' As she was going to get it, he called to her, 'Bring me a bite of bread, too.'

But she said, 'I swear by the Lord your God that I don't have a single piece of bread in the house. And I have only a handful of flour left in the jar and a little cooking oil in the bottom of the jug. I was just gathering a few sticks to cook this last meal, and then my son and I will die.'

But Elijah said to her, 'Don't be afraid! Go ahead and do just what you've said, but make a little bread for me first. Then use what's left to prepare a meal for yourself and your son. For this is what the Lord, the God of Israel, says: There will always be flour and olive oil left in your containers until the time when the Lord sends rain and the crops grow again!'

So she did as Elijah said, and she and Elijah and her

son continued to eat for many days. There was always enough flour and olive oil left in the containers, just as the Lord had promised through Elijah. (1 Kings 17:10-16)

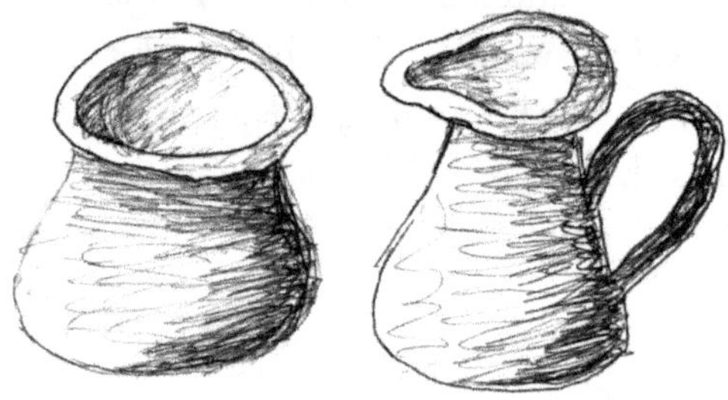

Invisible

The crowd pressed in around Jesus, but he stood his ground and kept his eye on John. So many people had come. It was incredible, just like he had been told. His heart beat quickly. It was almost time. It was really happening.

John stood tall and still, scanning those gathered. He didn't look at Jesus. Not yet.

'What gives you the right to baptise people?' a man asked John from the crowd. John didn't hesitate.

'I baptise with water, but right here in this crowd is someone you do not recognise. Though his ministry follows mine, I'm not even worthy to be his slave and untie the straps of his sandal.'

Hushed whispers spread through the crowd. People looked around at each other, trying to figure out who John spoke of.

'Did he say it's someone who is here right now?' a woman hissed to her husband. They stood close to Jesus. The women's husband nodded in response and they both peered around, curious.

Nobody knew that John spoke of Jesus. Nobody except for Jesus. Jesus remained still and quiet.

It wouldn't be long now. It was about to begin.

John told them, 'I baptise with water, but right here in the crowd is someone you do not recognise. Though his ministry follows mine, I'm not even worthy to be his slave and untie the straps of his sandal.' (John 1:26-27)

Nate

Nate sat beneath the fig tree and leaned back against the trunk, slipping off his sandals to feel the grass between his toes. The sun was shining, and he had a lot to think about.

It was hard to get his head around what he'd seen earlier that day. Nate had been close to Ammiel their entire lives. Nate had never imagined his brother could commit such a crime. Or that Nate would ever find himself in a situation like this.

He'd caught Ammiel in the act. There was no doubt in his mind about it. Ammiel had been stealing from their own father. Nate didn't know how long it had been happening or how much money Ammiel had taken. But he knew what he'd seen. He'd seen it with his own eyes, and he couldn't believe it.

Ammiel had tried to justify his crime. He'd used every excuse under the sun to explain why he'd taken the money. That only made it worse. It would have been better if Ammiel had shown remorse.

Nate could see through all his justifying. Nate alone knew how hard his father had worked in their family business over the years. The countless hours and sleepless nights. Ammiel didn't know. He was younger than Nate. Younger and ignorant.

Ammiel hoped Nate would keep his secret. But no matter which way Nate looked at it, he could not justify keeping

Ammiel's theft to himself. It was so clearly wrong, so black and white.

Nate gazed up through the branches of the fig tree to the blue sky above. He liked to come here to be alone. The fig tree was a good place to think.

Nate was torn. He didn't want to come between his brother and his father – their relationship was volatile enough as it was. But at the same time, he knew his conscience wouldn't let him keep this secret. Nate valued his integrity, a lesson he'd learned well from their father.

An hour passed. Nate was in deep thought and had come to a decision. He'd known the answer before he'd even arrived. He would go and tell their father. He had to. Ammiel would have to face the consequences of his actions. It was the only way and the right thing to do.

'Nate, there you are!' Philip sat down beside him on the grass. 'I've been looking for you everywhere.'

'Hey, Phil.' Nate sat up to greet his friend. 'Why were you looking for me?' Philip's eyes were bubbling with excitement. He had Nate's full attention.

'We have found the very person Moses and the prophets wrote about! His name is Jesus, the son of Joseph from Nazareth.'

Nate had not expected those words to come from his friend's mouth. 'Nazareth? Can anything good come from Nazareth?'

Philip laughed and shrugged. 'Come and see for yourself.'

Nate followed Phil to his feet and questioned him about Jesus as they made their way into town.

The men walked side by side, and Philip pointed down the road ahead of them.

'That's him,' Philip said, pointing to a man standing with

a small group of men off to the side of the road. He looked ordinary, but something inside Nate stood to attention. He felt nervous about meeting this Jesus.

Jesus turned to face them as they approached. He waved to Philip and smiled at Nate.

'Now here is a genuine son of Israel – a man of complete integrity,' Jesus said as they approached. Nate stopped in his tracks. How could Jesus know this about him?

'How do you know about me?' Nate asked.

Jesus smiled at Nate and he looked into his eyes.

'I saw you under the fig tree before Philip found you,' he replied.

Looking into Jesus' eyes, Nate got the feeling Jesus somehow knew what had happened with Ammiel. Did he know about the stolen money and the hard decision Nate had wrestled with under the fig tree? His spirit bubbled up within him, feeling as though it might burst from his chest.

'Rabbi, you are the Son of God, the King of Israel.' The words were strong but even as Nate spoke them, he felt the truth behind them. Jesus laughed.

'Do you believe this just because I told you I had seen you under the fig tree?' He shook his head and stepped forward to pat Nate on the back of his shoulder. 'You will see greater things than this.' He pulled Nate towards him and embraced him. Nate knew his life would never be the same.

Philip went to look for Nathanael and told him, 'We have found the very person Moses and the prophets wrote about! His name is Jesus, the son of Joseph from Nazareth.'

'Nazareth!' exclaimed Nathanael. 'Can anything good come from Nazareth?'

'*Come and see for yourself,*' *Philip replied.*

*As they approached, Jesus said, '*Now here is a genuine son of Israel – a man of complete integrity.*'*

'*How do you know about me?*' *Nathanael asked.*

*Jesus replied, '*I could see you under the fig tree before Philip found you.*'*

*Then Nathanael exclaimed, '*Rabbi, you are the Son of God – the King of Israel!*'*

*Jesus asked him, '*Do you believe this just because I told you I had seen you under the fig tree? You will see greater things than this.*' (John 1:45-50)*

Lonely Miracles

His mother smiled.
'Do whatever he tells you,' she said to the servant girls.
We know the Bible stories about him.
But she knew others.
Many others.
She knew the power her son possessed.
He was her child before he was our Saviour.
Some miracles she witnessed alone.

The wine supply ran out during the festivities, so Jesus' mother told him, 'They have no more wine.'

'Dear woman, that's not our problem,' Jesus replied. 'My time has not yet come.'

But his mother told the servants, 'Do whatever he tells you.' (John 2:3-5)

Tili

Tili was a tilapia fish, and he lived in the depths of the Sea of Galilee. He lived with his family and friends, and their families and their friends, and so on and so forth. There were many tilapia fish in the Sea.

Tili and his family did their business at night. They would scurry up from the depths in search of food, schooling and feeding through the hours of night when the moon shone bright. And during the day, when the sun came up, Tili and his family would disappear down to the deep, where they would wait out the daylight hours in safety. Tili was content with his simple life beneath the sea.

The tilapia fish knew their creator. Tili had heard his voice before, and knew who he was.

Tili enjoyed the nights of schooling with the other tilapia fish. Tonight, he had fed well. Now it was time to head back down to the depths.

It was dark and cool down below, and Tili rested with his family while the sun shone bright up above. Then a peculiar thing happened. There was a voice.

'Now, go out where it is deeper and let down your nets to catch some fish.' It was the creator's voice. Tili had heard it before and would never forget the sound.

The voice called to the tilapia fish, calling Tili and his family and all the other families up out of the depths. The voice told them to move towards the surface. The words didn't make sense to Tili. He'd never gone to the surface during the day before – it wasn't safe. But at the same time, he understood what the creator's voice called him to do. Looking around at his family and friends, it was clear they understood as well. It was the most unusual thing that had ever happened in Tili's life.

The tilapia fish swam swiftly and courageously, united in their direction. They swam through the water, following the creator's voice.

'Now, go out where it is deeper and let down your nets to catch some fish.' The words grew louder and clearer the closer they drew to the surface. Then Tili saw something sitting on the top of the water – it was large and floated on the surface, with an object swaying in the water beneath it.

Tili stopped and watched the interesting object as it swayed back and forth below the surface of the water.

Tili got the feeling he had a choice to make. He could go back down to the safety of the depths. Or he could follow the sound of the creator's voice burning inside his chest, calling him forward and telling him not to fear. Calling him into the swaying object. Tili knew he had a choice and while he didn't understand the creator's words, he had an overwhelming desire to follow his lead. The creator had placed Tili in the ocean to begin with. Surely he knew best. Maybe Tili would see his face if he followed his voice.

The tilapia fish were called into the large net beneath the boat and they willingly obeyed the voice of their creator.

When the net was pulled from the water and back into the boat, Tili lay on the floor, surrounded by his family and friends. He was out of the water and helpless, but he waited and listened.

'We need help,' a man called out over the water. Before

long, another boat stood beside them and was also filled to the brim with tilapia fish.

'Oh, Lord, please leave me. I'm too much of a sinner to be around you.' A man fell to his knees beside where Tili lay and held his head in his hands. Other men stood beside him, looking at Tili and the vast number of fish lying around him, and they shook their heads in disbelief.

'Don't be afraid!' It was the creator's voice. Tili instantly calmed when he heard him speak. Tili was safe as long as he was near. He lay still and listened. The creator stood right beside where Tili lay.

'From now on, you'll be fishing for people.' His face shone in the sunlight and was everything Tili imagined it would be. With a heart full of hope, Tili closed his eyes.

When he had finished speaking, he said to Simon, 'Now go out where it is deeper, and let down your nets to catch some fish.'

'Master,' Simon replied, 'we worked hard all last night and didn't catch a thing. But if you say so, I'll let the nets down again.' And this time their nets were so full of fish they began to tear! A shout for help brought their partners in the other boat, and soon both boats were filled with fish and on the verge of sinking.

When Simon Peter realised what had happened, he fell to his knees before Jesus and said, 'Oh, Lord, please leave me – I'm too much of a sinner to be around you.' For he was awestruck by the number of fish they had caught, as were the others with him. His partners, James and John, the sons of Zebedee, were also amazed.

Jesus replied to Simon, 'Don't be afraid! From now on you'll be fishing for people!' And as soon as they landed, they left everything and followed Jesus. (Luke 5:4-11)

Herod

King Herod had tossed and turned all night but had finally come up with a plan. He'd been infuriated at being outwitted by the wise men. They had met with him weeks ago, when they arrived in town, telling Herod they were searching for the newborn king. Herod had almost choked. But he'd managed to hold it together while he met them. He'd even convinced them that he, too, would like to find the newborn king to worship him.

He'd really been consumed with jealousy. Just the thought of a rival – newborn or not – made him wild. He would take every measure to protect his dynasty.

He'd come up with the plan sometime between the third and fourth hour of the morning and it was a good plan. He had the two pieces of vital information he needed. The wise men had been foolish in trusting him with the information. Perhaps they weren't as wise as they seemed. He chuckled to himself.

He had an idea of the timeframe of the child's birth. The wise men had seen a star rise, and they'd seemed sure the star symbolised the king's birth. Herod also had an idea of where the child was born. The star had guided the wise men here, and Herod had learned it would lead them on to Bethlehem. That was all he needed. When and where. Now he would take things into his own hands.

He called for Rono as soon as day broke.

Rono walked in briskly, almost tripping over himself. Herod kept a straight face, although he was slightly amused.

'Rono, I have a new decree.'

Rono pulled out his pen and papyrus, ready to take down Herod's instructions.

'All of the boys in Bethlehem and the surrounding area, under two years old, will be put to death. Immediately.' Rono went pale as he noted Herod's words.

Herod enjoyed a full breakfast in peace that morning for the first time since learning about the child's birth. He had outwitted the wise men. He had ruined the ancient prophecies about the child. He felt very clever.

The infant king would be dead by the end of the week. Perfect!

Jesus was born in Bethlehem in Judea, during the reign of King Herod. About that time some wise men from eastern lands arrived in Jerusalem, asking, 'Where is the newborn king of the Jews? We saw his star as it rose, and we have come to worship him.'

King Herod was deeply disturbed when he heard this, as was everyone in Jerusalem.

Then he told them, 'Go to Bethlehem and search carefully for the child. And when you find him, come back and tell me so that I can go and worship him, too!'

When they saw the star, they were filled with joy!

They entered the house and saw the child with his mother, Mary, and they bowed down and worshiped him...

When it was time to leave, they returned to their own country by another route, for God had warned them in a dream not to return to Herod.

Herod was furious when he realised that the wise men had outwitted him. He sent soldiers to kill all the boys in and around Bethlehem who were two years old and under, based on the wise men's report of the star's first appearance. Herod's brutal action fulfilled what God had spoken through the prophet Jeremiah. (Matthew 2:1-3, 8, 10-12, 16-17)

The Meeting

Jesus was alone now.

He left his disciples to watch, but they fell asleep. He dropped to his knees and fear coursed through his veins.

'Father, please help me. Is there any other way that it can be done?' The fear came in great waves, rolling over him one after another and his sweat fell to the ground like giant drops of blood.

The night was silent and still, his breathing the only sound. A light breeze blew his hair. He was a child looking to his father, afraid, looking for help, comfort, and reassurance. Looking for eyes that loved him.

And his Father came to him, to comfort his Son. They met alone, his presence surrounding where Jesus knelt and his words washing over him.

'I am with you. I believe in you. We've been talking about this moment for a long time. You've got this. I'll be here. I won't leave you. I love you.'

They went to the olive grove called Gethsemane, and Jesus said, 'Sit here while I go and pray.'

He took Peter, James, and John with him, and he became deeply troubled and distressed. He told them, 'My soul is crushed with grief to the point of death. Stay here and keep watch with me.'

He went on a little farther and fell to the ground. He prayed that, if it were possible, the awful hour awaiting him might pass him by. 'Abba, Father,' he cried out, 'everything is possible for you. Please take this cup of suffering away from me. Yet I want your will to be done, not mine.'

Then he returned and found the disciples asleep... (Mark 14:32-37)

Mave

Mave and Javan were well-respected members of the Nazareth community, held in high regard by the people. Their opinions mattered, and they knew it. Mave wasn't pleased when they arrived home this evening, and she knew Javan wasn't either. They didn't speak about it, but it just didn't sit right.

Mave tidied up their living quarters and prepared for bed, but she couldn't stop thinking about their day at the synagogue.

Mave had been shocked to silence along with Javan and all their family and friends. They had watched Jesus, whom they had known their entire lives, open little Tommy's eyes.

Tommy was nine years old and was popular among the children and was a friend of Mave and Javan's youngest son. But there had never been any question about Tommy's eyesight. His eyes had been broken since the day of his birth. He was completely blind.

Mave had helped Tommy find his way around or led him to find his mother countless times over the years.

And this day, this very morning, Jesus had touched Tommy's eyes and they had been opened. Mave could see Tommy's face now, the utter disbelief as he looked into Jesus' eyes. They were the first eyes Tommy had ever seen. Mave still couldn't believe it.

She slowly climbed the steps to the rooftop to find Javan. He was sitting in his favourite chair, staring out into the darkness.

'I can't believe Tommy can see.' He shook his head. He'd read Mave's mind.

'Neither can I,' she replied as she sat beside her husband. They sat in silence for some time.

'What do you make of it?' Javan spoke first. He didn't need to explain himself. Mave knew exactly what he meant. They had watched Jesus grow up from a young boy. No doubt about it, he'd grown into a fine young man. But who was he to perform such a miracle? And where did his incredible power come from?

'I don't know.' Mave shook her head. 'But there's something strange about it …' She couldn't put her finger on exactly what it was. 'Something about it just doesn't sit right.'

Javan nodded. She was relieved to see her husband felt the same way and was encouraged to continue.

'Where does he get this wisdom and the power to perform miracles?' she asked.

'I've been asking myself the same question all afternoon,' her husband replied.

Mave felt a deep unrest in her spirit. Should she stop speaking of these things? She couldn't. They welled up inside her, making their way to the surface.

'He's just the carpenter's son,' she finally said. 'And we know Mary, his mother, and his brothers – James, Joseph, Simon, and Judas.' She counted them off on her fingers. 'All his sisters live right here among us.' She'd said it. And it was the truth. Javan and Mave's own children had had the same upbringing as Jesus, so why should he be filled with such extraordinary power?

'Where did he learn all these things?' she asked. Her question hung in the air between them. Javan was silent for some time, and Mave waited for her husband to speak.

'I don't like it,' he finally said.

Then they were in agreement. They would make it clear to their community that they were not fans. Mave and Javan were not followers of Jesus.

He returned to Nazareth, his hometown. When he taught there in the synagogue, everyone was amazed and said, 'Where does he get this wisdom and the power to do miracles?' Then they scoffed, 'He's just the carpenter's son, and we know Mary, his mother, and his brothers — James, Joseph, Simon and Judas. All his sisters live right here among us. Where did he learn all these things?' And they were deeply offended and refused to believe in him... (Matthew 13:54-57)

Max

It had been a long day at work. Now Max sat on the end of his bed, staring at the folded white garment on a stool in the corner of the room. He'd won it fair and square in a game of dice at work.

But the events following the prisoner's death now made him uneasy. Max was trying to make some sort of sense of what had happened that afternoon.

He usually managed to leave work behind when he walked into his home, switching roles from Roman soldier to husband and father. This evening he'd felt different. He couldn't relax. He had rushed through mealtime, skipped over storytelling with his children, and escaped to his room to be alone.

He couldn't shake the feeling that something unusual had taken place, perhaps something significant. The sun had disappeared that afternoon following the crucifixions. It had become dark, as though nightfall had arrived hours too soon.

Max had never seen anything like it. But it was more than the strange darkness. Max had seen the prisoner's eyes. There'd been something about him, the one they called Jesus. Max didn't know what it was. He'd found it hard to look away from those eyes. He'd felt a familiarity there, which he knew was impossible. He'd certainly never met the man. Something stirred within Max when he looked into Jesus' eyes. Something Max couldn't put his finger on.

It was obvious the fellow had committed a serious crime,

one deserving punishment by death, nailed to a tree. Max was just doing his job … wasn't he? He had done it before, and he would do it again.

Max stood, shaking his head, trying to clear it. Enough was enough. What choice had he had? He would have been punished himself if he'd disobeyed orders. And why would he have risked his own life to defend a stranger?

He left the room, tired and ready for bed. He hoped Tally would join him. Max prepared for bed, cleaning his feet, changing his clothes, and checking in on his sleeping children. The white garment caught his eye each time he passed. It jolted his memory back to the afternoon on the hill. Was it whiter than it had been earlier? Glowing, even? That was impossible! He was letting his imagination get the better of him. Max jumped into bed. He needed to sleep and forget about his absurd day at work. But after tossing and turning in bed for some time, he decided to move the prisoner's garment out of his sleeping room.

Tally now slept beside him, so he got up quietly and stepped out into the courtyard. He carried the prisoner's garment with both hands and sat on a stool holding it before him, perplexed at the way that he felt, almost as though he wanted to cry. Max never cried. What had come over him?

He brought the garment to his face and inhaled the musky fabric that the prisoner would have been wearing only yesterday.

Tally stepped from their sleeping room into the courtyard. Max dropped the garment onto the table in front of him.

'What are you doing? Can't you sleep?' Tally looked from Max to the garment.

Nothing got by his wife.

'What is that?' she asked.

'It's nothing.' Max tried to play it cool. 'Just something I won at work today'.

After they had nailed him to the cross, the soldiers gambled for his clothes by throwing dice. (Matthew 27:35)

Purpose

Jesus sat at the wooden desk. The hours had passed quickly, and his family was asleep. The candlelight flickered across the scrolls laid out before him.

He was now a young man and he felt the Spirit's presence speaking to him more and more as the years went by. Revealing the secrets of creation, like the pieces of a puzzle falling into place.

He knew who he was now. He knew he was his Father's Son and who his Father was. He understood that he would save humanity from their sins … but how?

As the hours passed by, deep into the night, his tears fell, dripping onto the scrolls before him. His path was becoming clearer. His spirit was on fire with the truth, and his destiny was laid out bare before him.

He understood now why the plan had been drip-fed to him, piece by piece. He wouldn't have understood when he was younger.

He would carry the weight of the cross for his Father and for creation. For the greatest love this world would ever know. He would gladly take part in the plan his Father had constructed.

This was his calling. He felt it burning in his chest. He'd known it was there, but now, he understood.

Jesus grew in wisdom and in stature and in favour with God and all the people. (Luke 2:52)

Lemon

Lemon enjoyed her job. She was a professional mourner and was one of the best in the business. But there were times it was harder than others, and today was one of those times.

The deceased girl was young and Lemon had been fetched to support the family in their grief. She'd packed her bag and hurried to their home.

A man rushed past as she stepped through the front door, almost knocking her over. He didn't stop or apologise, but ran off down the road.

'I'm sorry.' A woman with red puffy eyes stood inside the door.

'You must be Tamar,' Lemon said.

'Yes.' The woman nodded, and Lemon embraced her. She couldn't imagine what it would be like to lose a child.

'That was her father,' Tamar whispered. What? Where would he be going? Why would he leave his family at a time like this? Lemon pulled back from Tamar but left her hands firmly on her shoulders.

'I'm here now. I will help you.' It was all Lemon could say to comfort the grieving mother. And it was the truth. Lemon was excellent at what she did. She would see that the funeral went as smoothly as it could.

The house was filling fast, and Lemon recognised other professional mourners among the guests. She got straight to work. She checked on the deceased child first. Her body was laid out on her bed, surrounded by flowers.

Lemon got busy leading the people in their mourning. She began with weeping, falling to the ground and holding her hands to her head. Those around her stopped in respect. All eyes were now on Lemon.

They watched her in silence until one by one, women in the crowd joined her, and they all wept together.

Lemon was skilled in her technique of wailing. She knew there was no one in attendance who could lead the funeral song like she could. And so she began, slowly at first, in short bursts. As she got going, she felt the familiar pounding in her chest and her love for the job took over. Lemon was swept away in the presentation of leading the grief.

The people in the home flocked to her and took her lead until it was a great uproar of weeping, wailing and wild body expressions. Tamar did not join in as the mothers often did. Instead, she sat by the door and held her head in her hands. Lemon kept one eye on her as she wailed. Wasn't she pleased with Lemon's work?

From what Lemon could gather, Tamar had no other children. Lemon felt angry at Tamar's husband. He'd run off to who knows where when it was clear his wife needed him.

Lemon snuck out for some water. It was important to keep up her fluids. Her throat would need to hold up for hours into the night. She wanted to speak to Tamar. Lemon needed to make sure her employer was pleased with her work.

Lemon placed a hand on her shoulder. Tamar didn't move but continued to hold her face in her hands.

'Tamar,' Lemon whispered. Tamar looked up, her face as pale as a ghost.

Lemon regretted interrupting her but she just needed to

make sure. Perhaps Tamar would like a different mourning style. Lemon could tone it down if she preferred.

'I wanted to ask if you're pleased with my work. Or if there is something else I can do for you.'

Tamar shook her head. 'It is good. Thank you.' She rested her face back into her hands.

That was all Lemon needed to hear. She prided herself on one hundred percent customer satisfaction and didn't want any complaints. Lemon got straight back to work. No longer worried about her employer, she led the people to an even greater level of mourning than before. The sound from Tamar's home was so loud it could be heard many streets away.

'Get out!' A male voice yelled, interrupting Lemon mid-wail. What? Lemon opened her eyes to see Tamar standing beside two men, one of whom was Tamar's husband. The other was a stranger Lemon hadn't seen before. It was he who had addressed the crowd with his shocking request.

Lemon stood to face the man. Tamar looked worried and Lemon wasn't sure what to say. Had this man really told the house full of mourners to get out?

The stranger looked at Lemon. All eyes were on him. What was going on? Why were Tamar and her husband not saying anything?

'The girl isn't dead. She's only asleep.' He spoke to the crowd, but his eyes held Lemon's. Lemon looked around the room at those beside her and then back into the stranger's eyes. Was he crazy? She laughed, and the crowd laughed with her.

'Of course she's dead, sir,' Lemon replied. 'We wouldn't be here otherwise. See for yourself.' Lemon pointed to the room where the girl lay.

Tamar's husband joined the stranger in ushering the people

outside. Lemon couldn't believe it. She slipped between the men to speak directly to Tamar.

'What is going on? Do you want the people to leave?' Lemon was ready to tell the stranger that he ought to be the one to get out. But Tamar slowly nodded. It seemed even she wanted the crowd to leave her home.

Lemon had never been to a funeral like this before. She was both offended and intrigued at being asked to leave. Most of all, she wanted to be sure she would still be paid for her work.

The people stood outside, each as confused as one another. Their hushed whispers suggested Tamar and her husband must be losing their minds in their grief.

Lemon sat down in the shade to rest. She would wait a while. The stranger would see the child was indeed dead. Then Lemon would be called back inside to resume her work. It was certainly an interesting interruption.

There were gasps and a woman screamed. What was happening? Lemon jumped up and followed the gazes of those around her.

The child, the dead girl, was standing at the door of the house.

Her parents stood beside her, one to each side, their faces a mixture of shock and wonder and fear. Their daughter was alive.

Lemon pushed through the crowd and reached out to touch the girl's arm. She had been dead. Lemon had seen her with her own eyes. Now she lived.

What on earth had happened in that room?

As Jesus was saying this, the leader of a synagogue came and knelt before him. 'My daughter has just died,' he said, 'but you can bring her back to life again if you just come and lay your hand on her.'

When they came to the home of the synagogue leader, Jesus saw much commotion and weeping and wailing.

'Get out!' he told them. 'The girl isn't dead; she's only asleep.' But the crowd laughed at him. After the crowd was put outside, however, Jesus went in and took the girl by the hand, and she stood up! The report of this mira-cle swept through the entire countryside. (Matthew 9:18, 24-26; Mark 5:38)

Morax

Morax could feel him before he actually saw him, and Morax was shocked!

What was he doing here? Why would the Son of God be inside a human body, in a house on earth? More importantly, what did this mean for Morax and the comfy home he'd made for himself inside his human? The further his human stepped inside the house and towards God's Son, the more Morax panicked. He needed to do something, fast. So he threw his human to the ground in protest and then he screamed.

'You are the Son of God,' he howled.

'Quiet!' A voice spoke. It sounded loud to Morax, although Morax could tell that those around them could not hear it.

Morax stopped then and looked at Jesus, and a great fear welled up inside of him. Would he get out of this alive? He didn't know, but if he was evicted from his home, he wouldn't go easily. He would only leave kicking and screaming.

Morax tried to call out again. He would expose God's Son to all those gathered in the house. He would tell them all who he really was. Morax had seen him before, but not in this world. It had been in another time and another place. Morax was sure it was him.

But Morax was silenced. His voice would not come out – it was little more than a whisper when he spoke. He was furious. He flung his human to the left and to the right. Those around him tried to help him, to hold him down, but they were not strong enough for Morax.

Suddenly the Son of God stood close beside him and held his face right up, within inches of his human home. The Son of God reached out his hand and touched him.

'Leave,' he spoke to Morax. And Morax had no choice. He instantly departed his home in silence and without any more protesting. That was it. There was no point in arguing further.

He had no hope, standing up against God's only Son.

As the sun went down that evening, people throughout the village brought sick family members to Jesus. No matter what their diseases were, the touch of his hand healed every one. Many were possessed by demons; and the demons came out at his command, shouting, 'You are the Son of God!' But because they knew he was the Messiah, he rebuked them and refused to let them speak. (Luke 4:40-41)

Perry

Perry had never fit in with the other teachers of religious law. He'd always had different ideas and often had to hold his tongue when it came to certain subjects. He'd made the mistake of speaking up about his ideas in the past and had been reprimanded by his colleagues. It seemed no one else in Perry's line of work agreed with the way he thought about things.

The other teachers didn't like Perry's ideas and they didn't like Perry. No matter how hard he tried to fit in, they looked down on him. They'd already made up their minds about him. In their opinion, Perry was lacking.

Perry had listened to a new teacher yesterday. His name was Jesus, and Perry had heard his very own ideas spoken out loud. Perry had been transfixed and his chest had burned with the truth he'd heard in the teacher's words.

Perry's colleagues had been in the crowd as well. They were far from impressed – he'd been able to tell by the look on their faces. They had scowled at Jesus. But Perry had listened. He had understood Jesus' teaching. Jesus spoke about things Perry had always pondered over, the ideas he could never share.

Perry wanted to go back to listen to him today. He'd thought of nothing else all night. Perry had questions. Who was Jesus? Where had he come from? And why wasn't he afraid to speak out about his new ideas, the way that Perry was? Perry didn't know … but one thing was for sure: Jesus' teachings aligned with Perry's innermost thoughts and beliefs.

By the time Perry arrived to listen to Jesus, there were many others gathered around him. Perry's colleagues were there, already speaking with Jesus. They, like Perry, had most likely been pondering over his teachings throughout the night. As Perry made his way further into the room, he realised his colleagues were questioning Jesus. Trying to outsmart him, no doubt.

'Your mistake is that you don't know the Scriptures, and you don't know the power of God,' Jesus said loudly and clearly to Perry's colleagues. Perry held his breath and listened, unable to believe what he heard. They wouldn't take it well, being spoken to like that. He was eager to hear how the debate would pan out.

Jesus didn't stop there but continued speaking. He spoke well and didn't hesitate in telling the leaders exactly what he thought. How did he do it? Where did he get such wisdom?

Perry's colleagues were shocked to silence and Perry saw his opportunity now to ask his question, the question that he'd been contemplating all morning.

'Jesus.' Perry's voice cracked a little and sounded wobblier than he'd imagined. Jesus turned his attention towards him. Perry swallowed hard. All eyes were now on him as he cleared his throat. 'Of all the commandments, which is the most important?'

Jesus looked Perry in the eyes. His pulse was racing as he waited for Jesus to reply, and he could feel his colleagues' disapproving looks.

'The most important commandment is this,' Jesus said.

'Listen, O Israel! The Lord our God is the one and only Lord. And you must love the Lord your God with all your heart, all your soul, all your mind, and all your strength.'

Perry soaked up Jesus' words, so pleasing to his ears.

But Jesus wasn't finished. 'The second is equally important: Love your neighbour as yourself. No other commandment is greater than these.' Jesus nodded at Perry when he'd finished.

'Well said, Teacher. You have spoken the truth by saying there is only one God and no other.' Perry could see the other teachers of religious law snickering at him out of the corner of his eye. But his confidence had returned, and he didn't care. He'd never heard anyone speak like Jesus, and he wanted to tell him so.

'I know it is important to love him with all my heart and all my understanding and all my strength, and to love my neighbour as myself.' Perry paused. His colleagues weren't going to like this. 'This is more important than to offer all the burnt offerings and sacrifices required in the law.'

There. He'd said it. He'd laid his cards out bare on the table, in front of Jesus and his colleagues and in front of the large crowd who had gathered. Perry heard a gasp from the corner where his colleagues stood, then quiet murmuring.

But Jesus did a double-take at Perry.

Perry held his breath.

'You are not far from the Kingdom of God,' Jesus finally said.

Tears sprang to Perry's eyes. He smiled humbly and took a seat on the ground, joining the crowd to listen to whatever else Jesus had to say.

Realising how much the man understood, Jesus said to him, 'You are not far from the Kingdom of God.' And after that, no one dared to ask him any more questions. (Mark 12:34)

You don't measure us for perfection.
We can come to you just as we are.

*But you, O Lord, are a God of compassion and mercy,
slow to get angry and filled with unfailing love and
faithfulness.*
(Psalm 86:15)

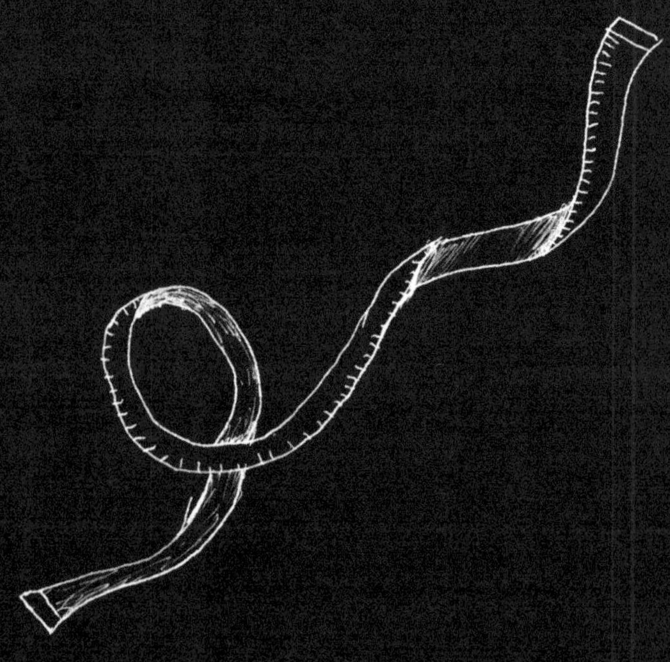

Mahli

Mahli and Dodo had a full house and were run off their feet. Mahli had let out their last available room to a young family. She was grateful for the work but relieved they would be welcoming in no more visitors. They had officially run out of space.

Dodo was already busy entertaining. He'd taken some of the men up to the rooftop to show them around. Mahli took the opportunity to rest for a couple of minutes. She placed a stool against the wall and sank into it, leaning her head back and closing her eyes. She would need to begin the meal preparations soon. She was pleased she would have help tonight from the women staying in their home. Children were gathering in the courtyard. They were shy but would be playing games in no time.

It had been a long day. Mahli had been up since not long after midnight, summoned to a neighbourhood home to help with a delivery.

Although Mahli and Dodo had no children of their own, Mahli had helped birth more babies than she could count. It was something she'd stumbled across accidentally and discovered she had a knack for it. Mahli's name was well known throughout Bethlehem as the woman to call on when it came to childbirth.

The town was overrun with visitors today, people returning to Bethlehem for the census. So Mahli hadn't had a chance to rest and recover during the day and her eyelids were heavy now.

'Are you sleeping?' a voice whispered. Mahli opened her eyes to find a young child standing just inches from her face. Mahli smiled.

'No, dear. Can I help you with something?'

'Could I please have a drink of water?' She was polite and very cute.

'Of course.' Mahli pulled herself back up from the stool. Just like that, her minute of peace was over. She didn't mind. Not really. Mahli enjoyed being busy and loved it when her home was full.

She rounded up a couple of young women from the court-yard to help with the evening meal preparations. Before she knew it, hours had passed by and they were almost ready to eat.

Mahli could hear Dodo and the visiting men as they made their way down the stairs. Their tummies would be rumbling with the food's aroma rising.

'How's it going, love?' Dodo stood beside her, water pitchers in hand.

'Almost there,' she replied. There was a knock at the door. 'Can you get that?' Mahli asked as she emptied the potatoes out onto a large dish before her.

She moved to the table where she began slicing the cucumbers. She could hear Dodo's conversation from where she stood. It sounded like someone else seeking lodging for the night. She heard Dodo apologise; they had no more room. A fresh-faced young girl popped up beside Mahli.

'Can I help you with that? I've nothing else to do.' She was enthusiastic, and Mahli was glad to hand her the knife.

'You can finish chopping the cucumbers if you like.' Mahli

moved across the room to wipe her hands and popped her head around the corner to the entrance. She was surprised to see Dodo still speaking to the people outside their door.

It was dark outside, and Mahli couldn't see their faces clearly but she heard a man's voice.

'Is there anywhere you could recommend we try? My wife is heavily pregnant and needs to lie down and rest.'

Mahli's ears pricked up. She took a candle from the table and joined her husband. He stood with a young couple who looked tired. They had obviously had a long journey.

'Hi, there. I'm Mahli.' Mahli smiled at the young mother-to-be.

'I'm Mary,' the young lady replied. She seemed shy but Mahli sensed a quiet confidence. 'And this is Joseph, my husband.'

'How have you been keeping?' Mahli asked. Her business hat was on now and she found every part of her profession genuinely interesting.

'I've been well, thank you,' Mary replied. 'A little sick at the beginning, but not too bad since.'

'You must be excited to find out if you're having a girl or a boy.' Mahli smiled.

'We're having a boy,' Mary replied. Mahli nodded politely. That was an answer she hadn't heard before. Obviously Mary meant they were hoping for a boy.

Mahli looked from Mary to Joseph, and her heart went out to the young couple. She had already made up her mind. Mary was close to having her baby – Mahli could tell from the size and shape of her belly.

She looked at Dodo. There was no way they could send them away. Dodo stared blankly back at his wife, saying without words that there was nowhere for them to go.

Mahli had an idea. It wasn't ideal, but it was warm. At least they would have privacy and a roof over their heads.

'What about the stable?' she whispered to Dodo, although she wasn't sure why she whispered as the couple could still hear her. Their hopeful faces flickered in the candlelight. Dodo shrugged and turned towards them.

'You're welcome to the stable if you would like it?'

And because Joseph was a descendant of King David, he had to go to Bethlehem in Judea, David's ancient home. He travelled there from the village of Nazareth in Galilee. He took with him Mary, his fiancée, who was now obviously pregnant.

And while they were there, the time came for her baby to be born. She gave birth to her first child, a son. She wrapped him snugly in strips of cloth and laid him in a manger, because there was no lodging available for them.
(Luke 2:4-7)

Pick Me

Jesus lay in his bed. It was early morning, just before daybreak, and no one else was awake.

He lay still, eyes closed, and he saw them – those he would choose. Fishermen beside the sea, at work for their father. A man beneath a fig tree, and another high up in a tree. One seated at his booth, a tax collector.

'Come, follow me. I will make you fishers of men. Come, follow me and be my disciple.' The words washed over him. He sensed no need to fear the men might not follow. Instead, he saw them each drop their task at hand, stand up, and take his lead.

More faces came, slowly moving before his mind's eye, one after another, and he learned their names. He would call them out of the crowd. Each one would step forward, would come to him on top of a mountain. He smiled to himself. It was all planned out – had all been thought of ahead of time. His Father was in control. It was almost his time now.

He would be ready.

Jesus called out to them, 'Come, follow me, and I will show you how to fish for people!' And they left their nets at once and followed him. (Matthew 4:19-20)

Oli

It had been a crazy few months, and Oli was feeling misplaced. It wasn't just that he had left the comfort of his home – or even that he missed Egypt. It was more that in leaving, Oli had left behind his purpose.

Oli knew it was odd how much he enjoyed his work. His friends would grumble and complain. They found building bricks repetitive, laborious and boring, but Oli had taken pride in his work. He'd taken pleasure in the whole process, from the formation of the mud right through to the finishing touches of the limestone veneer. His work had given him a reason to get up in the morning, a calling, a purpose. He had quickly learned that the way he felt about his work was unusual, that those around him did not share his love of using his hands to create.

That time in his life was over now. He'd been uplifted from the land of Egypt along with all the Israelite community. Oli had been filled with awe at the power of their God when they departed from Egypt. God had held his people by the hand and led them out. They'd wandered through the wilderness and camped before wandering some more.

Somewhere amidst their wanderings, Oli had discovered an unrest in his spirit. A yearning for the life he'd left behind, for meaning to his days, for the work he had treasured. He was filled with guilt about the way he missed Egypt. He hoped God could not see his yearning, that God would not be angry with him.

Oli stood in the crowd. Moses called them all from their tents and stood before them. Moses was the only person God talked to, so maybe he had a message from God. Oli waited in silence, watching their leader. His face shone, as it always did after he'd spoken with God.

Moses cleared his throat.

'People of Israel,' he called. Those who weren't watching turned their attention towards Moses.

'I have a message from our God.' Oli was right. Perhaps the message was something about their food or water, or perhaps an addition to their law. Oli waited patiently.

'God will live among us,' Moses called out. Incredible!

'God has given me detailed instructions about the home we must build for him so he can dwell among us,' Moses continued. He described an exquisite tabernacle, a sacred tent with covering clasps, frames, crossbars, posts and bases. An ark and its carrying poles and cover. A place of atonement, with an inner curtain to shield the ark.

There would be a table with carrying poles, utensils and a light, a lampstand and its accessories – lamp cups and olive oil. An incense altar and carrying poles. A curtain for the entrance of the tabernacle. The list went on and on.

Oli's heart beat harder and harder as he listened. Finally, the list was over. Moses stood, silent. Was he finished? No.

'We will take a sacred offering for the Lord. I want you to go back to your tents, and if you feel moved in your heart to present the following gifts to the Lord, then do so.' Moses went on to list what would be needed for the construction of the Lord's home, from gold, silver and bronze through to ram skins and gemstones.

Oli could see the people around him squirming with excitement. They were eager to bring their gifts to God, to have him in their midst to be near and protect them. Oli was excited as well.

Moses let the people go. Oli walked back towards his tent and he realised his excitement was for a completely different reason. Oli was excited at the thought of helping with the work.

Who would God appoint to build this creation for him? It would probably be Bezalel. Bezalel had an incredible gift of creating with his hands. Was there any chance, any possibility that Oli might be able to help? It was unlikely. Oli kept to himself and the leaders didn't know him.

Oli stepped inside his tent. He could approach Moses or Aaron and ask if he could help. But Oli didn't like making a fuss and it was hard to get an appointment with the leaders. Oli didn't know what he would say even if given the opportunity.

What would Oli give for the offering? He'd willingly donate anything if it meant God would stay with them. The thought of having God close by was comforting. The Israelites were vulnerable without a home or anywhere to call their own, and they needed God now more than ever.

It didn't take Oli long to decide what to give for the offering. While he rummaged through his belongings and added to his collection, he couldn't stop thinking about the work that would be done on the Lord's home, about God's detailed instructions to Moses and about the way he, Oli, might attempt to create the beautiful pieces.

Oli carried his pile of offerings to the gathering place where Moses stood. Oli waited his turn to lay down his offerings, adding to the already impressive pile of precious materials. Oli had no problem turning away from his belongings and leaving them for the building of the Lord's home. It was the right thing to do. Instead, he grieved for the work he had left behind and for his uncertain future. His hands ached to be busy and his mind would not quieten.

By the end of the day, the pile of offerings was astonishing. Oli was proud of his community.

Moses wept when he saw the collection, and the people kept coming, bringing their gifts late into the night. Oli watched from a distance before heading to his tent to sleep. He dreamed he was back in Egypt, but instead of creating bricks with his hands, he wove fine strands of gold and laid precious gemstones.

Oli woke early and lay in bed with his eyes closed, recalling his dream and the passion he'd felt while sleeping. But it had only been a dream. This was the worst part of his day – getting out of bed when there was no point, no purpose.

He had to get up, though, and go to the gathering place. Maybe he could talk to Moses or Aaron. Once again, the people gathered before Moses, their gifts for the building of the Lord's home towering behind him.

Moses cleared his throat before addressing the people. 'The Lord has specifically chosen Bezalel son of Uri, grandson of Hur, of the tribe of Judah. The Lord has filled Bezalel with the Spirit of God, giving him great wisdom, ability, and expertise in all kinds of crafts.'

Bezalel walked through the crowd to stand beside Moses. Oli had been right about Bezalel – he was a talented man. It made sense that God had chosen him.

'Bezalel is an expert in working with gold, silver, and bronze,' Moses said. 'He is skilled in engraving and mounting gemstones and in carving wood. He is a master at every craft.'

Oli knew these things to be true and he nodded his approval and admiration along with those who stood around him. Oli could imagine the pride and joy Bezalel must be feeling, standing there beside Moses.

Moses paused and looked out over the people, his eyes scanning the waiting crowd, back and forth. The people grew quiet. What would Moses say next? His eyes did not stop their searching … until they found Oli's. Oli held his breath. Could Moses really have been looking at him? Surely not. Perhaps he was looking at someone behind Oli. Were his eyes playing tricks on him?

Moses nodded and cleared his throat.

'And the Lord has given both him and Oli son of Ahisamach, of the tribe of Dan, the ability to teach their skills to others.'

Moses continued speaking, but Oli froze to the spot and his mouth hung open. Had Moses just called him by name? And named his father, Ahisamach? And his own tribe, the tribe of Dan?

'The Lord has given them special skills as engravers, designers, embroiderers in blue, purple, and scarlet thread on fine linen cloth, and weavers. They excel as craftsmen and as designers.'

Moses beckoned for Oli to join him. Those around Oli patted him on the shoulder as they made a way for him to walk through. He couldn't believe it. Had God seen him? Had he heard his silent pleas?

Oli joined Moses and Bezalel, who smiled at him. He realised his hands were trembling as he took his place beside Bezalel, and fear and wonder fell over him. His smile grew as he looked out at the sea of faces before him. He had been chosen. He would work again. This time, he would be building the Lord's home.

'The Lord has gifted Bezalel, Oli and the other skilled craftsmen with wisdom and ability to perform every task involved in building the sanctuary. Let them construct and furnish the tabernacle, just as the Lord has commanded.' Moses lifted his hands to the heavens. Oli closed his eyes, overwhelmed with thankfulness at being recognised, at being seen.

The Lord has filled Bezalel with the Spirit of God, giving him great wisdom, ability, and expertise in all kinds of crafts… And the Lord has given both him and Oholiab son of Ahisamach, of the tribe of Dan, the ability to teach their skills to others. (Exodus 35:31, 34)

Goldie

Goldie saw large gold gates up ahead. She seemed to float towards them although she wasn't sure how. Everything was silent, but she was safe. The streets were tidy inside, swept clean and peaceful.

She floated down quiet streets past many houses until she stopped in front of her house. She didn't know how she knew it was her home. She just did. Nowhere had ever felt so welcoming, so pleasing to her eyes. There was a deep familiarity. She could've sworn she'd been here before.

Goldie had a sense that the house had been designed with her in mind. Even from where she stood, she could see details in the home's structure and framework that she hadn't even realised she'd wanted.

Her hands ran over the white brick fence. It was perfect. She unlatched the gate as though she'd come home and knew it had been designed specifically for her hands. Somebody had thought of her, somebody who knew her well, who knew intimate details about her, who knew her even better than she knew herself.

Goldie stepped silently down the golden path leading to her front step. It was lined with sunflowers, her favourite, and daisies sprinkled the surrounding grass. She spotted a cherry blossom tree with a swing and a seat in the yard. It was like something out of a dream. She had never seen an outdoor setting so beautiful, so perfect, so her.

Her eyes filled with tears although she could still see clearly … so maybe they hadn't. But she was moved. When she arrived on her front porch, she noticed something in her hand and realised for the first time that she held a key. It fit the front door effortlessly, like a glove, and she opened up her home for the very first time.

And if I go and prepare a place for you, I will come back and take you to be with me that you also may be where I am. (John 14:3 NIV)

Si

Si was tired. It had been almost a month since he'd set out for Jerusalem. A month of long hot days walking and uncomfortable nights with little sleep. His excitement to see the city's towering walls up ahead made it all worthwhile. He had made it!

He wished his boys were with him to see its magnificence. He would bring them one day when they were older.

He imagined Jaalah now at home, with Rufus on her lap and Alex tucked beneath her arm. She'd be busy making their breakfast and getting them ready for the day. She loved their boys well, and he knew they were in safe hands when he travelled.

Anxious to arrive, he picked up his pace, stepping his worn sandals through the overcooked grass at his feet. He would get a new pair in Jerusalem. He was pleased they had survived the journey. Si was getting dangerously close to running out of travelling supplies. It was a relief to arrive.

As Si drew closer, he could hear the growing hum of people from inside the city walls. There would be hundreds of thousands inside, people who had travelled from near and far for the celebration. It was exciting to be a part of it.

Si's pouch grew heavy on his back. It was time to take a rest. But he was close now, and anticipation throbbed inside his chest. He'd push on. He continued walking towards the city entrance.

A loud voice hollered up ahead, and Si slowed down, cautious. He peered up at the entrance. A crowd of people streamed out from the city gates. Si was fast approaching them when he spotted a prisoner among the crowd. The prisoner was carrying the beam of a cross, and was surrounded by Roman soldiers armed with spears.

Si slowed down to watch the man. The prisoner tried to walk beneath the weight of the beam, but it was clear his steps caused him pain. He'd been beaten, and his clothing was soaked with blood.

What sort of crime had he committed to deserve such a punishment? It must have been something awful. The crowd was large, and Si wondered if he should wait until they'd cleared away from the entrance. But as he was eager to arrive, he decided to continue and make his way around them.

Si didn't want to look at the criminal or attract unwanted attention. He stole a glance as he walked past. The criminal was having great difficulty and wasn't going to get far with the cross on his shoulders. The torturing had clearly been taken too far. He wore a crown made of thorns, and his back was a mess. Si could only imagine the pain of the cross rubbing against it.

Suddenly the man fell beneath the weight. Si jumped back and slowed down beside him. His battered body lay in the dust. Si's initial reaction was to reach out and try to help him. But he stopped himself. It wasn't safe, and he was afraid to interfere.

'Get up!' A soldier kicked the prisoner in the side. The injured man remained silent as he tried to lift himself off the ground. Si saw his muscles strain and the veins in his neck bulging as he tried to get up. But the cross was too heavy, and he was too hurt.

Si glanced up at the soldier towering over his body and was surprised to see the soldier looking straight back at him. Si lowered his gaze and proceeded to move on by. To his horror, he felt the cold iron of a spear come down heavy on his shoulder. He stopped in his tracks and lifted his head to face the soldier.

'You carry his cross,' the soldier commanded.

Si was stunned. It was an order, and he clearly had no choice in the matter. He stole a glance at the sea of faces around him. Maybe somebody would help him. Maybe someone would offer to take his place. He saw only downcast eyes in the crowd, relief at not having been chosen.

Si wanted nothing to do with this situation. He didn't know the prisoner's name, his crime, or anything else about him. Why should Si have to carry the prisoner's cross? It wasn't fair. And when he was so close to Jerusalem!

'Come on.' The soldier led Si to the prisoner. He had made it onto his knees and was trying to stand. Si knelt beside him and reached for the beam. He glanced briefly at the prisoner's face, and breath caught in his throat when he looked into the prisoner's eyes.

His eyes were unlike any Si had seen before. Where Si had expected to see fear and misery, he saw determination, reassurance and peace. Si stared at the man, unable to look away. The peacefulness in his eyes had no place here; it seemed so foreign and misplaced.

Si blinked and shook his head as though waking from a dream. He couldn't believe what had become of this day, or what he had seen in the prisoner's eyes.

He lifted the cross, heaving it up over his shoulder. It was heavier than he'd imagined, much heavier than the pouch he'd grown tired of carrying only minutes earlier. The prisoner rose to his feet and the full extent of the damage done to his back was now evident. It had been ripped to pieces and Si's stomach turned at the sight.

'Hurry up,' a soldier yelled. The prisoner began to walk, following the lead soldier. Si followed with the cross. He kept his eyes low, looking at the path before his shoes. He could see the prisoner's blood-stained feet ahead of him, treading carefully.

Women followed then, wailing loudly. They must be close to the condemned man.

Was this an ordinary crucifixion? Were there usually so many people? Si had seen something unusual in the prisoner's eyes. Something alarming. He was surprised to discover that he felt great concern for the man wearing the thorn crown.

'Where are we going?' Si asked.

'Golgotha. Keep walking and keep quiet,' the soldier replied.

Golgotha? That didn't tell Si anything. They climbed up a hill. The soldier directed Si to drop the beam, to lay it down beside the prisoner. Si stepped back, his eyes downcast, and nodded at the prisoner. He had done as they'd asked.

He would leave now, as fast as he could. He'd pretend he had nothing to do with this. He took one last look into the prisoner's eyes and was drawn to them again. There was no doubt they were powerful eyes.

'Thank you, Simon.' The prisoner spoke in a voice so quiet that those around didn't even hear. But Si heard, and his feet froze to the spot.

The soldiers seized the man and threw him to the ground. Si watched as they took nails and hammered them through his flesh, his hands and his feet, nailing him to the wooden beam Si had carried. He couldn't look away as they pierced his skin and lifted him high. The prisoner had called him by name … and Si had told nobody his name.

A passerby named Simon, who was from Cyrene, was coming in from the countryside just then, and the soldiers forced him to carry Jesus' cross. (Simon was the father of Alexander and Rufus.) And they brought Jesus to a place called Golgotha (which means 'Place of the Skull'). (Mark 15:21-22)

Minni

Minni loved to cook and had been making preparations all morning for today's meal. There was no special occasion, but there didn't need to be. She had felt the need to make something delicious, so she would.

Minni had been to town that morning for supplies and planned to make a tasty lentil soup with flatbread and vegetables, and even something sweet for afterwards.

But by the time Minni arrived home, she was feeling unwell. She couldn't be sure, but she might be developing a fever. She placed her groceries on the table and sat down to remove her sandals. She would lie down for half an hour and see if she felt better after a rest.

She didn't want the food she'd purchased to go to waste. Minni pulled a blanket over her as she lay down on her bed mat. Had the temperature dropped? She felt cold. She closed her eyes and fell into a light sleep.

When she woke up, Minni was trembling and chilled to the bone. She definitely had a fever. Her heart dropped. Instead of getting a head start on her delicious meal, she had slept the day away and now felt awful.

She pulled her blanket up around her shoulders and hugged her knees to her chest. She should throw off the blanket and try to cool down, but she was so very cold. And her groceries were still on the courtyard table. Perhaps she could prepare the meal in small steps. If she could manage to chop a few vegetables, then she could come back to bed and rest. But she couldn't move, so she closed her eyes and remained where she was.

'Mother.' She recognised her son-in-law calling from the front door. 'I have some friends with me to visit. I hope that's okay.'

'I'm in here, Peter.' Minni's voice was raspy, and her head pounded with each word. She lay it back down on the cushion and waited. Peter poked his head into the room a few moments later.

'Mother, are you alright?' He stepped in and knelt beside her.

'I'm not well,' Minni whispered. Peter held his hand to her forehead then pulled back her blankets. Minni groaned but was too weak to protest.

'Peter, is everything okay?' a man's voice called from the courtyard. Peter took Minni's hand, holding it in his and kissed her cheek.

'Could I invite my friend in?' Peter whispered. 'He might be able to help you.'

What a coincidence. Peter's guest must be a doctor. She nodded her approval but kept her head on the cushion and her eyes closed. Even the daylight hurt them now.

One set of footsteps left the room, a minute passed, and two sets of footsteps returned. She heard them both kneel beside the bed mat. She trembled. It was cold without her blanket.

'Mother, this is my friend. His name is Jesus. Jesus, this is my mother, Minni,' Peter said.

Minni opened her eyes a little to greet the stranger. He had warm eyes.

'Hello, Jesus,' she whispered.

'Hello, Minni.' He reached out to touch her hand then paused. 'May I?'

'Yes.' Minni watched as Jesus took her hand into his. When his fingers touched hers, her trembling stopped. She took a deep breath and sighed it out, leaving her body completely still. The fever left, as though being lifted from her, and a deep calm settled over her body. Her head stopped pounding and was clear.

Minni opened her eyes wide and looked at her hand in Jesus' hand. Peter bounced on his toes, as though unable to contain something bubbling up within him. He looked from Jesus to Minni.

'How do you feel?' he asked, his eyes dancing.

Minni lay silent. Stunned. She didn't know what to say or what to think. What had just happened? Had it been a dream? Had she really felt so unwell just moments earlier?

'I feel good,' she finally whispered. 'In fact, I feel very good.'

Jesus helped her up from the bed and did not take his hand from hers until she stood beside them.

Minni looked from Peter to Jesus and laughed out loud. Both men laughed with her. She hugged them, Jesus first and then Peter.

'Thank you,' she said to Jesus as she followed the men out into the courtyard. 'Are you hungry?' she asked.

Her mind was reeling as she pulled the grocery items from her basket to prepare their meal. Who was Peter's friend Jesus? And how had he made her well with a simple touch?

When Jesus arrived at Peter's house, Peter's mother-in-law was sick in bed with a high fever. But when Jesus touched her hand, the fever left her. Then she got up and prepared a meal for him. (Matthew 8:14-15)

Almost There

Jesus on a donkey with coats thrown over its back.

Dust swirling high in the hot sun with all the commotion underfoot.

People everywhere, collecting branches and clothing to lay on the ground before him.

The voices of a large crowd talking and hollering, singing and clapping.

His legs rubbing roughly against the donkey's side.

Breathing dust, his smiling eyes, purpose-driven eyes, looking ahead of him on the road to the city.

Many in the crowd spread their garments on the road ahead of him, and others spread leafy branches they had cut in the fields. Jesus was in the centre of the procession, and the people all around him were shouting, 'Praise God! Blessings on the one who comes in the name of the Lord!' (Mark 11:8-9)

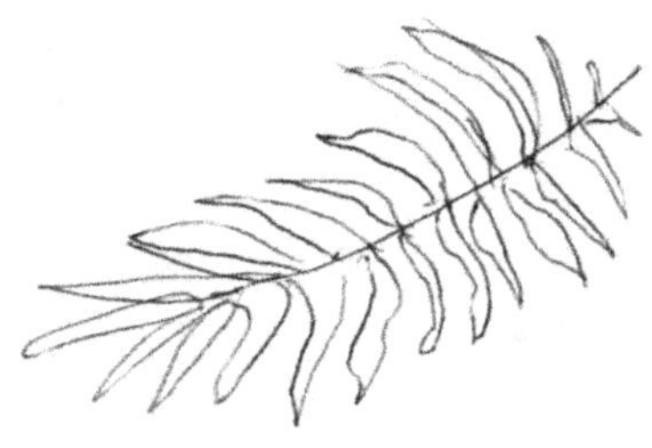

Tomas

Jesus pulled the twelve aside. They sat together on large rocks, away from the crowd.

'Listen, we're going up to Jerusalem.' He leaned in and spoke quietly so no one would overhear. 'All the predictions of the prophets concerning the Son of Man will come true. He will be handed over to the Romans, and he will be mocked, treated shamefully, and spit upon.'

Tomas looked around the small circle. Were the others following what Jesus was saying? There were blank stares all round. They looked as confused as Tomas was.

'They will flog him with a whip and kill him,' Jesus continued. 'But on the third day, he will rise again.' Jesus looked at each of them then, one at a time, and each man nodded. When his eyes met Tomas', Tomas nodded as well, although he wasn't sure what he was agreeing to.

Jesus stood and walked back to the waiting crowd. No matter where they went, a crowd would follow.

'Did you guys get any of that?' Tomas whispered under his breath. Jesus was still within earshot, and Tomas didn't want him to know he didn't understand.

'I have no idea what he's talking about,' Andy said, confirming Tomas' suspicion. They were all clueless. Sometimes the things Jesus spoke about made no sense whatsoever. Tomas puzzled over Jesus' words as he rejoined the crowd. He ran them over and over in his mind, trying to figure out their meaning. But it was no use. It was a mystery.

But they didn't understand any of this. The significance of his words was hidden from them, and they failed to grasp what he was talking about. (Luke 18:34)

Rueby

It was bound to be another wild night at Matt's. Rueby could hardly wait! She needed a drink – she'd already been sober for far too long – well, sober for the afternoon. In her books, that was far too long. It would be good to catch up with the crew too. She fitted in at Matt's. It was one of the only places she belonged any more.

Rueby had a new motto – if it was fun then she did it, and if it wasn't fun then she didn't. It was all about fun, pure and simple. So she partied her days away.

There had been a time when Rueby didn't live her life from one drink to another, but those days were gone. She'd buried them along with a world full of hurt and broken dreams. She no longer cared about the things of her past. Now she lived each day exactly as she pleased. A party girl, that's who Rueby was now.

Her mother's face flashed before her eyes and she stopped in the street. She hated it when that happened. Any reminder of her past was unwelcome. Especially memories of her mother, who would lecture Rueby about how she was hurting her body and soul in countless ways. A night at Matt's was exactly what she needed. She shook her head and continued walking. Nights at Matt's were the best. Rueby clutched her bottle of liquor and climbed the steps to his front door. She could hear the familiar music and smiled to herself. She entered without knocking, and Matt enveloped her in a giant hug.

'There she is.' Matt smiled and planted a kiss on her cheek. Rueby blushed, feeling shy. She needed a drink. 'Help yourself, Rueby,' Matt called after her. 'You know where the cups are.'

Rueby poured herself a large cup and carried her bottle to the table set up in Matt's dining area. She would keep the bottle close beside her because she would need it all.

Rueby scanned the guests seated around the table – it was the usual rowdy crowd, and she liked them all. They were a lot like Rueby. She saw Adah sitting on the other side of the room and made a beeline to sit beside her. Adah spotted Rueby before she'd made it round and jumped up to greet her.

'I was hoping you'd come,' Adah squealed. Rueby hugged her, and they sat down together. 'I was worried about you,' Adah said quietly when the girls were seated.

'Me? Why?' Rueby pretended she didn't know what Adah meant. Adah shifted uncomfortably.

'Well, after Zeph's party the other week. Do you remember?' Adah asked. Rueby didn't, but she'd heard about it. She'd assumed Zeph had been overreacting, but the look on Adah's face now got her wondering. Rueby had had a lot to drink at Zeph's, and it had been another messy night. She hadn't been able to remember if Adah had been there, but obviously she had. How many others present tonight had been there that night? Not too many, she hoped. She put on a smile and shrugged. She didn't want to talk about it. There seemed to be a larger crowd than usual. Rueby spotted a group of men that she'd never seen at Matt's before.

'Who are they?' she asked, pointing. Adah let her veer the conversation away from Zeph's party.

'Matt's had an interesting day!' Adah whispered. 'Have you heard of the teacher, Jesus? The one who has apparently been performing miracles all over the show? Well, he's here!'

Rueby's eyes widened. What would someone like that want at one of their parties? He was a teacher, a preacher, he taught about God. And they were … well, they were party animals. Sinners.

'I know! It's a bit weird.' Adah must have read Rueby's mind. She spoke to Rueby, but her eyes were on Jesus. 'I feel a little uncomfortable too,' she whispered.

Rueby swivelled around in her seat to scope out this 'Jesus'. He looked ordinary. He looked relaxed. It annoyed her that he was here. What was Matt thinking? Matt sat beside Jesus and some other men Rueby hadn't met before. 'The other men are Jesus' disciples, whatever that means!' Adah said.

Ordinarily, Rueby would be thrilled to have new men at one of their evenings. But not tonight. Not men who would likely judge someone like Rueby. Well, she would beat them to it. She picked up her bottle and stood.

'Where are you going?' Adah looked worried. Adah didn't drink as much as Rueby. She didn't need alcohol the way Rueby did.

'Watch this,' Rueby whispered narrowing her eyes. The alcohol was already doing its magic inside her head. She was well and truly relaxed now, much more like her new self. She walked straight up to where the men were gathered and pulled up a seat beside Matt.

'Rueby, meet my new friends!' Matt greeted her.

Rueby ignored him. 'Who wants to play a drinking game?' Rueby could tell Matt was sober, and none of the men wanted to play.

'Then I'll play alone.' She looked straight at Jesus and took her bottle to her lips. It was awfully unladylike, but she didn't care. She just wanted a reaction, wanted to send a message to Matt's visitors that they didn't belong and she would carry on as she always did whether they were around to judge her or not. She didn't lower her bottle until she'd emptied the entire thing. It should have lasted her hours, but it would be worth it to see the look on their snobby faces.

Their reaction wasn't what she'd expected. The men carried on their discussion, and Rueby found herself in the middle of a boring conversation between Matt and a couple of Jesus' disciples. Jesus moved away and was speaking to some people on the next table over. Probably trying to get away from Rueby. Some Pharisees soon joined the discussion at Rueby's table, and she began to feel very drunk. Just the way she liked it.

'Why does your teacher eat with such scum?' one of the Pharisees asked the disciples sitting beside Matt. Rueby couldn't believe her ears. She would have defended her friends if she'd been able to. She had plenty to say, but her head was spinning and she knew she might not be awake for much longer.

The seat beside her was no longer empty. When Rueby turned to look, Jesus now sat beside her. He looked angry. Why would he be angry? Was he angry at Rueby for drinking so much? But Jesus was looking at the Pharisees, the men who had asked such a rude question about Rueby and her friends. The Pharisees noticed his arrival and squirmed in their seats. Good. But why was Jesus angry at them? Maybe she liked him after all.

'Healthy people don't need a doctor,' Jesus didn't take his eyes off the men as he spoke 'Sick people do.' Jesus looked at Rueby then, but she didn't feel judged the way she imagined she might have. He looked at her with compassion in his eyes, and his look felt like it touched the things buried within her. Rueby thought she might cry.

'Now, go and learn the meaning of this Scripture.' Jesus turned back to the Pharisees. 'The scrolls say, "I want you to show mercy, not offer sacrifices." For I have come to call not those who think they are righteous, but those who know they are sinners.'

And with that Rueby's eyes closed and she toppled forward. She vaguely remembered being carried by a man who laid her on a couch and covered her with a blanket where she slept safely until morning.

As Jesus was walking along, he saw a man named Matthew sitting at his tax collector's booth. 'Follow me and be my disciple,' Jesus said to him. So Matthew got up and followed him.

Later, Matthew invited Jesus and his disciples to his home as dinner guests, along with many tax collectors and other disreputable sinners.

But when the Pharisees saw this, they asked his disciples, 'Why does your teacher eat with such scum?'

When Jesus heard this, he said, 'Healthy people don't need a doctor – sick people do.' Then he added, 'Now go and learn the meaning of this Scripture: "I want you to show mercy, not offer sacrifices." For I have come to call not those who think they are righteous, but those who know they are sinners.' (Matthew 9:9-13)

Direct Connection

Father, I pray for Simon Peter. I plead for him.
Thank you for the friendship you have given me in Simon.
Thank you for his stubborn devotion to me.
Would you restore his faith, and quickly!
Would you lead him to repentance after the rooster's third
crow and turn his heart back to me.
Father, please do not let the guilt hold him back, but let him
believe in your forgiveness. Let him push forward into all
you have planned for him.
Would he accept your grace, and return to me.
Father, make him strong and let him strengthen the others.
Lord, protect his mind from the evil one.

*'Simon, Simon, Satan has asked to sift each of you like
wheat. But I have pleaded in prayer for you, Simon, that
your faith should not fail. So when you have repented
and turned to me again, strengthen your brothers.'* (Luke
22:31-32)

Zeky

Zeky scuffed his sandals through the dust as he walked to the synagogue. He didn't feel like going today. The sun was shining, and he wanted to go swimming instead. But his parents insisted. They said he needed to attend, along with the other young men in their community.

'Zeky!'

He spun around to see Mac and the rest of the gang. Zeky waved out, pleased to walk to the synagogue with his friends. Mac caught up with Zeky first. 'That waterhole's looking good today.'

'You read my mind.' Zeky grinned.

'Another beautiful Sabbath in Capernaum spent sitting in the synagogue.' Mac winked at Zeky. Zeky laughed. He loved the synagogue, but sometimes he'd rather play! He was a young man now, and he longed for freedom. There was so much to do and see. At least Eva would be at synagogue. Zeky knew that he and many of the young males would spend a considerable amount of time pretending not to watch her.

Zeky had admired Eva since he was a boy. Now she had developed into a young woman, he thought of her more often than not. He hoped he'd be seated with a clear view of her today.

'Eva's family ate with us last night,' Mac said, as though reading Zeky's mind. Mac stopped and looked down at the trees lining the water's edge, and Zeky felt a rush of jealousy.

'Oh?' He tried to sound casual.

'Who is that down there?' Mac held one hand up to shade his eyes and pointed down through the trees.

Zeky didn't care who was down there. He just wanted to hear about dinner with Eva. But he stopped walking and looked down to the water's edge. There was movement in the trees. Something scurried from behind one tree to another. Was it a wild animal? Suddenly a blood-curdling scream rose up from the trees, and Zeky realised who it was.

'It's just Ahi.' Mac turned to continue walking. 'He's been bad lately. They say he might be possessed.'

'He's crazy!' Zeky said, but could think of nothing but Eva's dinner with Mac.

In the synagogue, Zeky sat with his friends, and could see Eva from his seat. She sat with other young women who whispered and giggled among themselves. Zeky found it hard to look away.

'Hey, Zeky.' Mac grinned. 'Who you looking at?' Zeky's cheeks heated, and he dug his elbow into Mac's side.

'She asked about you last night. Not that you'd be interested, right?'

'She did?' Zeky's eyes widened. He was finding it hard to keep his cool when it came to Eva. 'What did she say?'

'Excuse me.' A priest addressed the crowd, and all became silent. Zeky would have to wait until after the service. What had Eva asked Mac? Was it possible she felt the same way about Zeky as he did for her?

A man spoke to the crowd. Zeky recognised his voice, and he stretched around the person in front to see who it was – Jesus. Good. Jesus had been speaking at the synagogue a lot recently, and Zeky enjoyed listening to him. He wasn't boring but spoke with real authority, and Zeky remembered his words long after leaving the synagogue.

There was a loud shuffle at the back of the building, followed by the crash of something hitting the floor. Zeky and the rest of the crowd spun around. It was Ahi! He was standing in the doorway. Ahi's eyes were wild and his clothing was filthy. He looked terrifying. What was he doing here?

Ahi stepped into the room, his eyes on Jesus. Zeky turned back to see Jesus step down from the platform. The crowd was silent, all eyes on Ahi.

Ahi's breathing was heavy, and he clenched his teeth together. Could Mac have been right about him? Could he really be possessed? A shiver ran down Zeky's spine.

'Go away!' Ahi screamed and pointed his finger at Jesus. 'Why are you interfering with us, Jesus of Nazareth? Have you come to destroy us?'

How did Ahi know who Jesus was? And why would he accuse Jesus, the teacher, of wanting to destroy him? Zeky held his breath. Mac looked just as confused and raised his eyebrows at Zeky, but nobody spoke a word.

Jesus took slow, steady steps through the crowd towards Ahi. He did not seem afraid.

Ahi panicked more and more with each step Jesus took.

'I know who you are!' Ahi pointed to Jesus. Jesus drew nearer and nearer. 'You're the Holy One sent from God…'

'Be quiet,' Jesus said, his voice calm. He held up both hands, interrupting Ahi mid-sentence. Ahi was silent. Jesus looked into his eyes

'Come out of the man,' Jesus said.

Ahi was thrown to the ground. The people nearby leapt up and away from him. And then he was still. Ahi lay unmoving in the dust. Jesus knelt beside him and placed his hand on Ahi's back.

'What on earth was that?' Mac whispered. Zeky was surprised to see Eva and the other young women standing close behind them.

'I don't know,' Eva whispered. 'But who is Jesus? Are his words so powerful that even evil spirits obey them and flee at his command?'

The group stood in awe as they watched Jesus help Ahi to his feet. Ahi wept and held his face in his hands, and Jesus embraced him.

Then Jesus went to Capernaum, a town in Galilee, and taught there in the synagogue every Sabbath day. There, too, the people were amazed at his teaching, for he spoke with authority.

Once when he was in the synagogue, a man possessed by a demon – an evil spirit – began shouting at Jesus,

'Go away! Why are you interfering with us, Jesus of Nazareth? Have you come to destroy us? I know who you are – the Holy One sent from God!'

Jesus cut him short. 'Be quiet! Come out of the man,' he ordered. At that, the demon threw the man to the floor as the crowd watched; then it came out of him without hurting him further.

Amazed, the people exclaimed, 'What authority and power this man's words possess! Even evil spirits obey him, and they flee at his command!' (Luke 4:31-36)

In the middle of the storm, you hold my hand.
Though it rages all around me, you keep me calm.

'I am leaving you with a gift – peace of mind and heart.
And the peace I give is a gift the world cannot give.
So don't be troubled or afraid.'
(John 14:27)

Livi

Livi sat up in bed, her heart hammering against her chest. She inhaled deeply as she loosened her grip on the blankets and willed the fear away. It was only a dream. Just a bad dream. But unlike any dream she'd had in her life.

'Are you alright, ma'am?' Silla's voice startled Livi. Her maid stood beside the bed with a pitcher of water and a worried expression.

'Oh … yes. I'm alright … quite alright,' Livi said. 'It was just a bad dream.' She tried to shake it off with a fake smile and a little laugh. She accepted the water from Silla. 'Thank you. You may go.'

But Livi did not feel fine. The dream had been so lifelike, it was difficult to come back from. There'd been a man in her dream, and his face was crystal clear.

He'd been in some kind of trouble, and he was bleeding. It was just a little blood at first, but then there was more and more. The blood was everywhere. It came from numerous wounds and flowed from his body until it covered the ground where they stood.

He had needed Livi's help. But she hadn't known how to help, how to stop the bleeding or how to save him.

She hadn't been afraid of him. Rather, she'd reached for him. She'd wanted to comfort him. His blood covered her hands, and she'd held his head in her arms as it dripped from his face. She'd been so close to him; she'd watched him gasp for breath, the shallow lines on his forehead so clear. And then she'd woken up.

Livi lay back down, nestling into the pillows behind her.

She would have something to eat and prepare for the day. The dream was sure to leave her after that. If the dream was some kind of message from the gods, she didn't understand what it meant.

Livi stepped out into the sunshine with Silla close behind. It looked like a beautiful day in Jerusalem. The Passover festival was in full swing, and there were people everywhere!

Livi felt on edge. She couldn't shake the feeling her dream had left behind. Was there some unknown meaning behind it? She couldn't figure it out and hadn't thought of anything else since the minute she opened her eyes.

She could hear the crowds gathering in the public square outside her home. She would go and find her husband, confide her dream to him, and see if he had any insight. He would be working, but she was sure he would take a minute to speak with her.

The public square overflowed with people so Livi went to the back entrance. The guards moved aside as she approached, letting her by. She could hear the crowd shouting and hollering and knew her husband would be on the platform now, addressing the people.

She might have to wait to speak with him later.

Livi stood on the side of the platform and could see him sitting before the crowd in the seat of judgment. Silla wiped down Livi's chair and held it out as Livi sat down.

She turned her attention to the platform and noticed that her husband was not alone. Two men stood to either side of his seat, both in chains. It must be that time of the year, the time they released a criminal.

It was custom each year during the Passover celebration to release one prisoner to the crowd – the crowd's choice!

One criminal had his back towards Livi, and she could see he had already been beaten. There was blood on his clothing, and the sight of it took Livi back to her dream. She remembered the man's face as clearly now as when she had slept.

Livi took a deep breath. She would speak with her husband soon, after the prisoner's release. He would help her to figure out the meaning of the dream … or at the very least, help her to calm down.

'Which one do you want me to release to you?' Livi's husband called out. Just the sound of his voice helped to settle Livi's nerves. 'Would you like Barabbas?' he asked as he yanked the prisoner on his right to face the crowd.

'Yes, yes! We want Barabbas,' the crowd replied, almost instantly.

Livi recognised the prisoner from a previous trial. Barabbas was a murderer. And the people wanted him released? Why?

Her husband paused and looked out at the people. He looked troubled, but Livi didn't know why.

'Or do you want Jesus who is called the Messiah?' He pulled the man on his left to face the crowd and Livi saw the prisoner's face for the first time.

She gasped and held her hands to her mouth. It was the man from her dream! The blood rushed from her head. Livi leapt up and turned to face Silla.

'What is it, ma'am? Are you alright? You look like you've seen a ghost.' Silla moved to Livi's side and placed a hand on her shoulder. 'Sit, ma'am. I'll get you some water.' She ran off.

Livi wiped the sweat from her brow and tried to regain her composure – people were looking at her. She was afraid to take a second look at the prisoner, but she knew it was him in her heart. She was sure.

What could this mean? What would she do? How could this man have visited her dream?

Livi took a deep, steady breath and closed her eyes. She accepted the water from Silla and braced herself before looking back up to the stage. The man they called Jesus was hurt, and she was surprised by the way she felt for him. She remembered the way she'd held his head and the look of desperation in his eyes.

She must do something. She needed to warn her husband. She must try to help this Jesus. But even as she turned to call for Silla, she heard the crowd's voices rising.

'Crucify him, crucify him!' It was an evil chant, almost as though not of this world.

Her dream was a message! This man might not deserve to die, and if that was the case, she did not want his innocent blood on her husband's hands.

'Fetch me some paper and ink,' Livi demanded. She needed to get a message to her husband. Fast, before it was too late.

Livi's husband sat back on the judgement seat between the two criminals, in deep thought. Livi scribbled her note:

Leave that innocent man alone. I suffered through a terrible nightmare about him last night.

But when the leading priests and the elders made their accusations against him, Jesus remained silent. 'Don't you hear all these charges they are bringing against you?' Pilate demanded.

But Jesus made no response to any of the charges, much to the governor's surprise.

Now it was the governor's custom each year during the Passover celebration to release one prisoner to the crowd — anyone they wanted.

This year there was a notorious prisoner, a man named Barabbas. As the crowds gathered before Pilate's house that morning, he asked them, 'Which one do you want me to release to you — Barabbas, or Jesus who is called the Messiah?' (He knew very well that the religious leaders had arrested Jesus out of envy.)

Just then, as Pilate was sitting on the judgement seat, his wife sent him this message: 'Leave that innocent man alone. I suffered through a terrible nightmare about him last night.' (Matthew 27:12-19)

Matty

Matty was confused. He stood in his sleeping room with his bag open before him. He was trying to pack but was torn as to what to take. Surely he would need more than he had been instructed to pack. Yet every time he added an item to his bag, he felt convicted and took it back out.

He looked at the pile on his bed beside his bag – a couple of changes of clothes, an extra pair of sandals, and what remained of his last pay packet. He would definitely need money. He didn't have to use it. He could just carry it with him in case he got desperate. It seemed like the wise thing to do. Surely it wouldn't be a problem.

He stared at the coins for a moment longer before placing them inside his bag. Next, he turned to his clothing pile. After eyeballing it for a couple of minutes, he decided to split it by half. Just one extra set of clothes would do. Perhaps then it would sit better with him …

He placed his choice inside his bag and put the other set away. There! That should do it. He wiped his hands together and left the room. He was hungry and needed to eat.

Matty took some cheese and bread from the cabinet in the courtyard and fetched himself a cup of water. He tried to ignore the nagging feeling inside his chest as he sat down to the table to eat his snack.

He took a bite, but it sat in his mouth, dry and uncomfortable. He sighed loudly and jumped back up, leaving his snack on the table, and returned to his room to resume his packing. He removed the clothing and coin purse from his bag and stood, hands on his hips, staring at the empty bag. Would he be able to do this? Could he embark on such an adventure and take nothing with him?

He held one hand up to his forehead and massaged his temples, then closed his bag and put it away. He had never done anything like this before – it was way out of his comfort zone. It wasn't that he didn't trust Jesus. He did. Really. It was just that his overactive imagination wouldn't stop thinking of all the things that could go wrong. There were so many possibilities.

What if he spilt his food all over his only outfit? It had happened before. Or what if he was hungry and there was no food and no money? What if his sandals broke? He looked down at his feet. His shoes were new and still had years in them, but anything was possible!

How could he leave it all behind and trust that everything would be okay? Matty could feel the burning in his chest he was becoming accustomed to. Deep down, he knew he would be leaving home tomorrow with empty hands. It was only as he accepted the idea that he could successfully swallow his mouthful.

He ate the rest of his lunch, remembering the day a few weeks earlier when Jesus had healed a paralysed man. The look on the man's face had been unlike anything Matty had seen before. He remembered the blind man who had been given sight. He remembered the young girl who had died and how Jesus had given her life!

It was incredible, completely mind-blowing. Matty found his faith rising as he thought of all that had happened over the past few months. He smiled to himself.

He was honoured to be a part of this story. Surely it would go down in history. No one who had ever lived had done the things Jesus could do.

So Matty would do as he'd been commanded, even if his part was just a small part. Even if Jesus' instructions didn't make any sense. Even if it made Matty uncomfortable. He'd leave his traveller's bag where it was, packed away in his sleeping room.

He would embark on this journey for Jesus tomorrow with empty hands.

Jesus called his twelve disciples together and gave them authority to cast out evil spirits and to heal every kind of disease and illness.

Jesus sent out the twelve apostles with these instructions: 'Don't go to the Gentiles or the Samaritans, but only to the people of Israel – God's lost sheep. Go and announce to them that the Kingdom of Heaven is near. Heal the sick, raise the dead, cure those with leprosy, and cast out demons. Give as freely as you have received!

'Don't take any money in your money belts – no gold, silver, or even copper coins. Don't carry a traveler's bag with a change of clothes and sandals or even a walking stick. Don't hesitate to accept hospitality, because those who work deserve to be fed.' (Matthew 10:1, 5-10)

Judah

It was so unfair. Did God love her? Did he see her? Or perhaps he hated her?
Every day ached.

Leah's husband didn't love her. Instead, he loved her
younger sister. They flaunted their love in front of Leah. Some
days she wished she might die so she could end the pain. God
was with her husband Jacob. Jacob succeeded in everything
he put his hands to. And no doubt God would carry on his
promises through her sister's child. After all, Jacob loved
Rachel and he made no secret that he favoured her son.

What was the point of Leah's life? Would she always be
second-best? Unloved and unwanted?

'Mama.' Judah pushed the door to her tent aside. His little
knees were covered in dirt and his fists were full of flowers.
Leah turned to her son, her beautiful boy, and bent down to
scoop him into her lap. She planted a kiss on his plump little
cheek, and he smiled up at her as he offered his collection.

*Once again Leah became pregnant and gave birth to
another son. She named him Judah, for she said, 'Now
I will praise the Lord!' And then she stopped having children.* (Genesis 29:35)

The scepter will not depart from Judah, nor the ruler's staff

145

from his descendants, until the coming of the one to whom it belongs, the one whom all nations will honor. (Genesis 49:10)

Almo

Almo had only heard second-hand stories about Jesus, and he wanted to see for himself. He didn't expect to be impressed and certainly didn't expect to be converted. Almo was a teacher of religious law and knew full well that the people were being led astray. It was some sort of trickery, perhaps even brainwashing. Almo couldn't be sure until he saw for himself. He had come to see Jesus today out of contempt ... and a little curiosity.

Almo's wife, Jadah, had offered to come with him, but he'd heard horror stories of women led astray by Jesus. Almo wouldn't risk it. He'd told Jadah he wanted time alone, and it would be a good chance to take a stroll to town on his own.

He sat in the crowd now and listened as Jesus spoke. But Almo found it hard to understand a lot of what was said, although he wouldn't admit that to anyone. Jesus seemed to speak in riddles. His stories didn't follow the usual structure, and Almo struggled to make sense of them.

Almo didn't let his confusion show in his face. Instead, he concentrated on keeping his expression as neutral as possible. Jeiel entered the room and came to sit beside him. A look passed between them. Jeiel was also a teacher of religious law, and they were obviously here for the same reason.

Almo watched Jesus as he spoke. The man certainly wasn't what Almo had expected. Jesus was a simple man, dressed plainly. He spoke clearly, but Almo didn't understand the attraction. Why were hundreds of people streaming in each day to listen to this man? What did Jesus have that Almo didn't have? He didn't even make sense!

A young man with withered legs was lowered before Jesus. He lay on a mat and it was clear he was disabled. Almo sat straight up. This was what he'd been waiting for. He was sure the people reporting miracles must be exaggerating. Jesus was just a man, a trickster. Almo would watch him closely.

Jesus stood from his chair and knelt beside the young man's mat. He looked at the paralysed man as though in deep thought. The people around Almo were quiet now, and Almo realised he was holding his breath. That was silly! He quietly let it out.

Almo glanced at Jeiel, and Jeiel nodded back. Between the two of them, they would figure out what Jesus was up to.

Almo turned his attention back to Jesus, who still knelt beside the mat.

'Be encouraged, my child! Your sins are forgiven,' Jesus said to the young man.

Almo almost choked but managed to disguise it as a cough behind his hand. What was Jesus doing? Who did he think he was? Did he think he was God? That was blasphemy! Almo returned Jeiel's furious expression.

Both men glared at Jesus. What would he do next? Jesus stood beside the mat and looked straight out into the crowd and straight into Almo's eyes! Almo inhaled sharply, and Jesus held his gaze. Almo looked back at him and shifted uncomfortably. Jesus then looked from Almo to Jeiel and back again.

'Why do you have such evil thoughts in your hearts?' Jesus asked.

Almo froze. How could Jesus have known their thoughts? Had their expressions betrayed them? Almo couldn't be sure, but Jesus' eyes pierced through him and he swallowed nervously.

'Is it easier to say, "Your sins are forgiven" or "Stand up and walk"?' Jesus asked. Almo didn't answer and neither did Jeiel. Where was Jesus going with this?

'I will prove to you that the Son of Man has the authority on earth to forgive sins.' Jesus looked straight at Almo and Jeiel as he spoke. Then he turned his attention back to the young man lying before him.

Almo watched the paralysed man's face for the first time since he'd arrived. He was crying.

'Stand up, pick up your mat, and go home,' Jesus said to the man. Jesus spoke so quietly that Almo had to strain his ears to hear him. Almo held his breath again. He'd never heard a silence like the silence that followed Jesus' words.

The young man on the mat jumped up to his knees, then straight onto his feet. The people gasped, and a woman screamed. Almo froze and watched.

He watched as the young man leapt up and down, punching the air with his fists. He watched as the young man wrapped his arms around Jesus' neck and then leaned down to roll up his mat. He watched as the young man laughed and cried and danced with those standing around him.

Almo didn't look at Jeiel. He couldn't. Instead, he stood and left the room. What in the world had just happened? How would Almo explain this to Jadah?

And who was Jesus?

Some people brought to him a paralysed man on a mat. Seeing their faith, Jesus said to the paralysed man, 'Be encouraged, my child! Your sins are forgiven.'

But some of the teachers of religious law said to themselves, 'That's blasphemy! Does he think he's God?'

Jesus knew what they were thinking, so he asked them, 'Why do you have such evil thoughts in your hearts? Is it easier to say "Your sins are forgiven," or "Stand up and walk"? So I will prove to you that the Son of Man has the authority on earth to forgive sins.' Then Jesus turned to the paralysed man and said, 'Stand up, pick up your mat, and go home!'

And the man jumped up and went home! Fear swept through the crowd as they saw this happen. And they praised God for giving such authority to a man! (Matthew 9:2-8)

Jemima

Jemima had been flirting with one of the governor's soldiers for weeks. She'd heard through the grapevine that his name was Jeri. It suited him.

Jemima had finally plucked up courage to speak with him this morning. She'd asked if he would like a cold drink. He had replied with a playful grin and asked her name. Jemima hadn't been able to wipe the smile from her face all morning.

The other servant girls were teasing her. They jabbed their elbows into her ribs when they walked past the soldiers. Jemima could feel her cheeks redden and hoped Jeri hadn't noticed.

'Jemima, come here please.' Lydia's words snapped Jemima from her thoughts. She entered the food preparation courtyard.

'Did you want me?' Jemima asked.

'I thought you might like to carry these out and wait on the soldiers this morning.' Lydia winked at Jemima.

Jemima felt her cheeks grow hot again.

'I'll take that as a yes.' Lydia handed Jemima a tray stacked high with bread and fruit before Jemima had a chance to reply.

Jemima was pleased. She'd take any opportunity to serve the soldiers, especially when Jeri was working.

'They're in their headquarters,' Lydia called after her. Jemima's heart quickened at the thought of seeing Jeri smile at her again.

Once outside the courtyard, Jemima placed the tray down and ran her fingers through her hair. She straightened her uniform and pinched her cheeks before picking up the tray again.

She could hear the soldiers' voices echoing down the corridor, hooting and hollering. It sounded like they were having a great old time.

She was surprised to see so many soldiers as she stepped out into the sunshine. It looked like the entire regiment was there. Was it a special occasion? She would need more food!

She placed the tray down on a table and made her way around the yard, staying close to the brick wall. She carefully stepped around a bramble plant growing against the wall. She'd been cut by brambles before and had learned to steer clear of their thorns.

She edged her way around the yard until she finally caught a glimpse of what the commotion was about. The soldiers had a criminal in the centre of the courtyard. By the looks of it, they were having far too much fun torturing him.

He was covered in blood and they had stripped off his clothes. He stood naked as the soldiers cursed him and laughed in his face. Jemima felt sorry for him; it was hard to look away.

Jeri emerged from the crowd and headed towards Jemima. Her heart leapt in her chest. She shifted her attention from the prisoner to Jeri's handsome face. But he didn't speak to her. Instead, he knelt and pulled at the bramble.

'Be careful with that,' Jemima said. Jeri smiled at her, and she blushed. Without saying a word, he took a blade and used it to cut off a branch which he wove around on itself until it formed a perfect circle. Jemima couldn't figure out what he was doing.

'A crown for the king,' Jeri called out to the rowdy crowds. He took the thorn branch and pushed it down onto the prisoner's head, piercing his skull. Blood poured out from the wounds, running down his face and into his eyes. The soldiers hooted with laughter, encouraging one another on.

Jemima didn't like it. Her breakfast curdled in her stomach.

Another soldier held up a scarlet robe. 'He's a king, isn't he?' That set the men off again, their laughter echoing off the high stone walls.

The soldier took the robe and placed it around the criminal's shoulders. It fell over his head, and he sank back into it. Jemima wanted to help him; she wanted to make the torturing stop. The inside of the robe was the only corner he had – the only place he could hide. Jemima watched as he clutched the robe from the inside and held it tight.

Jeri placed a large stick in the prisoner's hand. The soldiers knelt before the prisoner, mocking and taunting him as if the stick was a sceptre and he was their king. Tears pricked the corner of Jemima's eyes. She swallowed with difficulty over the lump in her throat and tried to blink away the tears.

'Hail! King of the Jews!' a soldier yelled. Jeri stood and spat in the man's face. The saliva dripped down through the prisoner's eyes, mixing with the blood.

Jeri leaped forward, grabbed the stick from the prisoner's hand and struck him over the head. The prisoner hit the ground, and dust flew into the air. The robe fell around him, covering where he lay. The soldiers exploded in laughter so loud that Jemima wanted to block her ears.

'Get up!' a soldier demanded. The prisoner tried to lift himself beneath the heavy cloak but struggled to stand.

His robe fell back from his head, and Jemima saw the man's face as he watched those around him. There was a tenderness in his eyes. He looked nothing like the criminals she'd seen in the past.

Jemima winced at the frightened look in his eyes. She didn't want to see anymore. She turned to leave. She needed to get out of there, fast. She walked briskly towards the entrance but stopped when somebody grabbed her arm. Jeri.

'Where are you going?' He grinned. 'You'll miss the show.'

'I don't want to see the show.' Her eyes filled with tears and her voice trembled. She was shocked at how the torture affected her.

She turned and walked away from the courtyard, the soldiers, and Jeri. She was no longer interested in anything he had to offer.

Some of the governor's soldiers took Jesus into their headquarters and called out the entire regiment. They stripped him and put a scarlet robe on him. They wove thorn branches into a crown and put it on his head, and they placed a reed stick in his right hand as a scepter. Then they knelt before him in mockery and taunted, "Hail! King of the Jews!" And they spit on him and grabbed the stick and struck him on the head with it. When they were finally tired of mocking him, they took off the robe and put his own clothes on him again. Then they led him away to be crucified. (Matthew 27:27-31)

The key to your presence is thankfulness.
So why do I begin with requests?

Enter his gates with thanksgiving;
go into his courts with praise.
Give thanks to him and praise his name.
(Psalm 100:4)

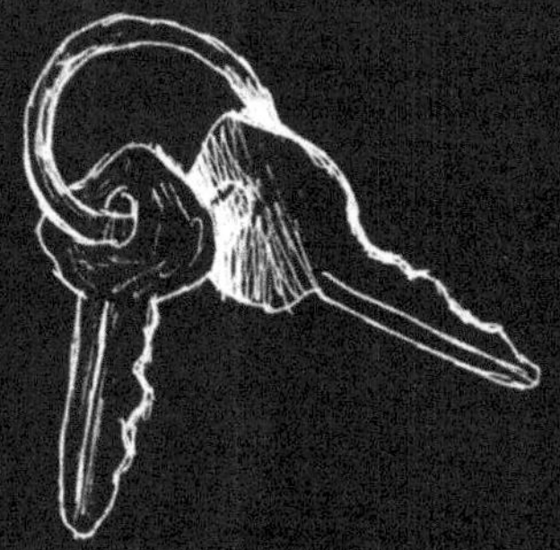

Joseph

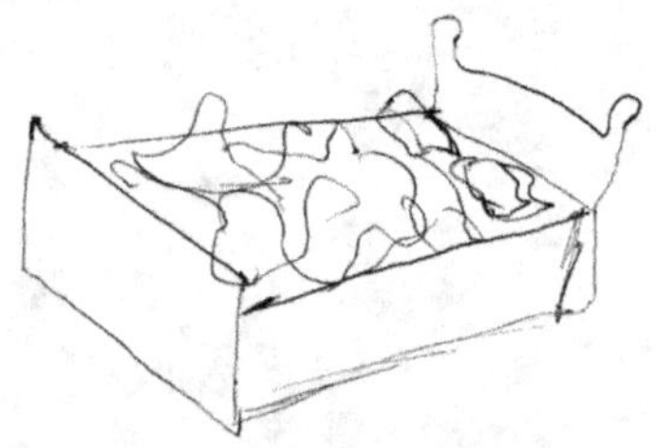

Joseph woke up with a start. He lay still, his breathing coming in quick hard gasps as he stared at the dark ceiling. He had only ever had one dream like that before. He remembered it well. It was when he had been sure that Mary had cheated on him. She had told him she was pregnant, and it wasn't to him even though they were engaged to be married!

Joseph had been devastated, sure he would no longer marry her. But then he'd had the God dream. An angel had spoken to him, so clearly, and assured him the child Mary carried had no human father but was God's own child. Mary was still a virgin. Joseph had believed. It had all happened the way God had said it would, and Mary had given birth to their son, who they had named Jesus.

But now the angel had visited him again. This message was alarming.

'Get up! Flee to Egypt with the child and his mother. Stay there until I tell you to return, because Herod is going to search for the child to kill him.' Joseph did not doubt this time. He was sure the angel had brought a message from God.

Mary lay beside him, deep in sleep. She would be tired. She'd only just got Jesus back to sleep after feeding him an hour or so before. He would need to wake her. He'd need to wake them both. They needed to leave.

'Mary,' he whispered, squeezing her shoulder. 'Mary!' He tried again, a little louder.

'What is it?' Her eyes remained closed, but she was listening. He wasn't sure how to tell her without frightening her. He'd just have to say it.

'God sent me another dream.'

Mary opened her eyes then and rolled over to face him. 'He has?'

Joseph nodded. 'We need to leave. Tonight.'

Mary sat up in bed and Joseph relayed the full message to her. It was a dark night, but they would leave now. They had to. They got up and packed their belongings into a bag, just what they could carry. They left Jesus sleeping until the last minute.

It was eerie, being up while the rest of the town slept around them. They whispered in hushed voices and stayed as quiet as they could. They would tell no one where they were going. By the time anyone noticed they'd left, they would be well on their way to Egypt.

They stepped outside where it was cooler. Mary cradled Jesus to her chest as the clouds parted, letting the moon light the road before them. Just like that, their lives were uprooted.

Anything to keep their boy safe from harm.

After the wise men were gone, an angel of the Lord appeared to Joseph in a dream. 'Get up! Flee to Egypt with the child and his mother,' the angel said. 'Stay there until I tell you to return, because Herod is going to search for the child to kill him.'

That night Joseph left for Egypt with the child and Mary, his mother. (Matthew 2:13-14)

Straight Street

It happened on Straight Street. It was a road Ananias knew well, but he'd never walked it so full of fear before. He had to obey the instructions given him, but he couldn't keep his mind from wandering. What if he was arrested today? What if he was taken in chains far from his home? There was even the possibility of death – what if he was killed?

The thought made him dizzy, and he stopped walking. He stood still in the middle of the road, feet glued to the spot, looking ahead past the long row of houses. He could see why the street had been named Straight Street. It was the first time he'd had the thought. He remembered playing on the road as a child with his friend Nekoda. He'd lived a few doors down, and they'd spent endless summers playing ball here on the road. Ananias had fallen over on Straight Street and grazed his knee. It had hurt a lot, and if he looked hard enough, he could still find the scar.

The house of Judas where he must go to deliver his message was just up ahead. Ananias wiped the sweat from his brow, pushed the hair back from his face, and tucked it behind his ears. His hands trembled, and he hid them in his tunic. He prayed a silent prayer to the one who had sent him here. Ananias would trust him. It was all he could do.

He put one foot in front of another until he arrived at the door of the house of Judas. He didn't need to call out on his arrival as a man met him almost instantly.

'Can I help you?' he asked.

'Yes. My name is Ananias, and I am looking for a man named Saul.' Ananias spoke bravely and held his head high. There was no turning back now.

The man's eyes widened, and he ushered Ananias inside without another word, leading him straight to a dimly-lit room where a man lay on the bed.

'Ananias is here,' the man said as he led Ananias in. The man on the bed sat straight up, holding both hands on either side of the bed to steady himself, and cried. Ananias froze, shocked. Was this really Saul? The man he had heard so many stories about? The man he had feared for all these months? Here he sat, crying uncontrollably on the bed.

Ananias stood still for only a minute, taking it all in. Then he leapt into action, full of confidence in his God. It was just as he had been told and he knew exactly what he needed to do. Saul was blind – although his eyes were open, it was clear he could not see. Ananias stepped forward, sure of himself as he placed his hands on Saul's shoulders. Saul calmed down.

'Brother Saul,' Ananias said. 'The Lord Jesus, who appeared to you on the road, has sent me so you might regain your sight and be filled with the Holy Spirit.' Ananias removed his hands from Saul and watched his face as his eyes were opened. Saul blinked once, twice, three times, then leapt from the bed and wrapped his arms around Ananias. Ananias patted his back, still not quite believing this was the man he had so feared.

'What should I do now?' Saul asked as he released Ananias from his firm grip. Ananias paused for only a second.

'I will baptise you,' he replied. Saul nodded, and the men walked from the room together.

Now there was a believer in Damascus named Ananias. The Lord spoke to him in a vision, calling, 'Ananias!'

'Yes, Lord,' he replied.

The Lord said, 'Go over to Straight Street, to the house of Judas. When you get there, ask for a man from Tarsus named Saul. He is praying to me right now.

'I have shown him a vision of a man named Ananias coming in and laying hands on him so he can see again.'

'But Lord,' exclaimed Ananias, 'I've heard many people talk about the terrible things this man has done to the believers in Jerusalem!'

But the Lord said, 'Go, for Saul is my chosen instrument to take my message to the Gentiles and to kings, as well as to the people of Israel. And I will show him how much he must suffer for my name's sake.'

So Ananias went and found Saul. He laid his hands on him and said, 'Brother Saul, the Lord Jesus, who appeared to you on the road, has sent me so that you might regain your sight and be filled with the Holy Spirit.' Instantly something like scales fell from Saul's eyes, and he regained his sight. Then he got up and was baptised. (Acts 9:10-13, 15-18)

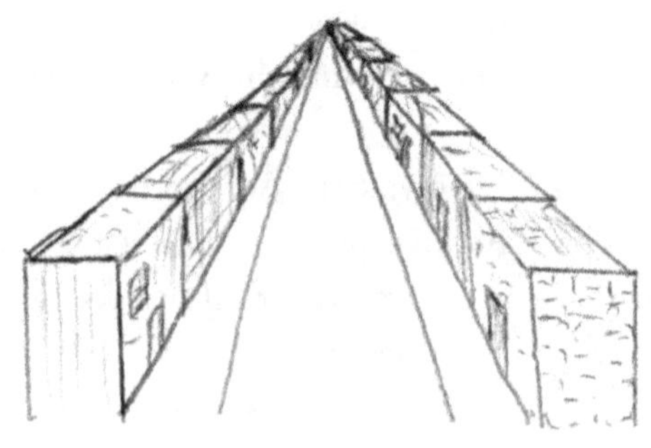

Bart

Bart lay in bed, staring up at the ceiling. He couldn't sleep. Those had definitely been his words. He was sure of it. Jesus had specifically said, 'Go into ALL the world and preach the good news to everyone.'

But how would they ever do that?

Yes, they were his disciples! Sure, they had travelled with Jesus. They'd witnessed countless miracles. They'd even assisted him by performing miracles themselves, in Jesus' name. But beneath it all, they were a bunch of unruly characters. They were just men! An odd group of ordinary men. The task was too big.

The 'whole world' seemed far-fetched. Out of reach. Was it even possible for a message, even a message as important as this one about God's own son, to reach every place in the entire world? What would happen when Bart and the other disciples were no longer alive? Who would continue on with their message? How would it survive?

Eighty years down the track, when the disciples of Jesus were no more, would it fade out into oblivion? Would anyone even remember Jesus?

Bart knew it wouldn't stop him from trying. Nothing could hold him back from trying.

He tossed and turned in his bed. Sharing the message was important, and Bart felt the weight of the command on his shoulders.

Jesus was who he said he was. Bart knew that without a doubt. He'd seen Jesus leave the earth and be taken up to heaven. Bart was ready to sacrifice his whole life to spread the news about Jesus. He would go anywhere and do anything.

As the hours crept by, a soft whisper washed over Bart, a voice he was becoming accustomed to. It spoke of truth persevering through the test of time. It spoke of reassurance and encouragement. Bart let the words wash over him, listening, and welcoming them.

An understanding took hold in his spirit. If Jesus was God's son, if that was the truth, then no matter how much time went by, and no matter how many generations passed away, Jesus' message would live on. It would reach the end of the world. Nothing would be able to stop it.

If God had created the world, then he would be able to keep the message of his son alive until the end of time. Bart just had to do his own small part, and spread the message burning in his heart. He could trust God to do the rest.

And he told them, 'Go into all the world and preach the Good News to everyone.' (Mark 16:15)

Peni

Peni and Ira sat on their rooftop. They sat in a comfortable sort of silence, one formed over decades spent in each other's company. They sipped their hot drinks and rested their weary feet. The fields stretched out before them and the sun made its way towards the horizon.

Ira grunted, waking himself from a light doze. It was time for them to head indoors. Peni stood with hands on both sides of her seat to steady herself. The years had been kind, but her balance wasn't what it used to be.

'Come on, dear.' She squeezed her husband's shoulder. 'Let's head to bed.'

Ira grunted and slowly rose to his feet.

'I'll just check on the animals,' Peni said as she made for the stairs down from the rooftop.

It was dark now, but Peni knew her way well, down the track to the field where the animals slept. She found Sol under the olive tree where he waited for her each night. Peni nuzzled her wrinkled face into his mane and cackled to herself. He seemed to enjoy their cuddles as much as she did. Sol was a donkey, but Peni believed he had become as fond of her as she was of him.

She had sensed a tenderness in his nature from the moment she'd met him. Although young, Sol wasn't one to push or make a fuss among the other donkeys. Ira had shaken his head when Peni relayed her feelings for Sol. But Ira knew how much she loved their animals, and was never surprised when she found herself another favourite.

Wishing Sol goodnight, Peni kissed him between the eyes and hobbled back up toward their home.

Ira was up at the crack of dawn, and Peni could hear him shuffling about in the courtyard. He knocked things over as he moved around their humble living quarters.

Peni had dreamed of Sol, dreamed somebody had been riding him, but she couldn't see who. Peni missed riding. It had been an odd dream, so lifelike. It had woken her up, and she'd stayed awake for hours afterwards.

Peni had come to the decision in the wee hours of the morning that it was time Sol was broken in. He'd been ready for a while, and she wasn't sure what held her back from having him ridden.

She shouldn't be riding at her age, so she would get one of the workers to break him in. But Peni loved Sol and wanted to do it herself.

Peni ate in a hurry, then went down to the fields to lead Sol up to their front door. She left him tied there as she went about getting ready for the day.

'You've got a spring in your step.' Ira sounded suspicious as he leaned against the doorframe. 'Is there a reason Sol is parked up at our front door?'

Peni braced herself for the inevitable argument. She smiled at her husband. 'Sol's ready to be ridden, and I want to be the one to ride him.' Ira shook his head.

'It's not safe, Peni. I thought we'd agreed your riding days were over.'

But Peni was determined and stood her ground. Sol needed to be ridden and she would ride him.

Peni stepped out into the sunshine to draw water for Sol.

She understood Ira's concern for her safety and loved him for it, but she wanted to ride Sol, even for a short while. She pulled the water up from the well and turned to head back inside when she noticed two men heading towards their house.

She didn't recognise them. They must be from out of town – probably seeking directions. Peni wrapped her arms around the water jar and followed them up to her front door.

One of the strangers walked right past the front door and headed straight towards Sol. Peni could hardly believe her eyes as she watched the man reach for the ropes holding him.

'Excuse me,' she called, panic rising. The men jumped. She had taken them by surprise.

'Why are you untying my donkey?' She tried to remain calm. The man who held Sol's rope dropped it and stepped back, clearly nervous. He looked from Peni to his friend.

'The Lord needs it,' he finally replied. Four simple words. But they came back to Peni as she lay in bed that night.

Something inside of Peni had shifted when they were spoken. Sol would be ridden that day but not by her. She could explain it no more than she could understand whom the strangers spoke of.

She had known it was right, though. She'd felt it. Perhaps there had been a meaning behind her dream?

Peni had surprised herself in her response to the strangers. She'd simply nodded. She'd stood there, clutching the water jar, silently watching as the men untied her pride and joy and walked him out of the village gates.

The Lord needed Sol. Who was she to stand in the way?

'Go into that village over there,' he told them. 'As you enter it, you will see a young donkey tied there that no one has

ever ridden. Untie it and bring it here. If anyone asks, "Why are you untying that colt?" just say, "The Lord needs it." (Luke 19:30-31)

David

David ran as fast as he could. He ran as though his life depended on it. He could hear their voices, and they were closer now than they had ever been in all his months of hiding.

Their voices echoed around him, bouncing from one mountain to another.

Fear surged through his body, pushing him on until suddenly he stopped and crouched behind a large rock. He panted hard, needing to catch his breath. He couldn't be sure exactly what direction the voices were coming from.

He shifted his pouch, adjusting it over his shoulder, and wiped his brow. His heart beat so hard against his chest that he could hear it ringing loud in his ears. He remained as still as he could, listening.

A minute passed by, then he heard them again. So close this time, he knew he'd be in trouble in a matter of minutes if he didn't move. They were tracking him down, hunting him like a deer.

He needed help fast. He peered out from around the rock and took a quick sweeping scan of his surroundings. Which way should he run? It was a tough decision, an important decision. He spotted a small cave tucked into the mountainside. The cave mouth was partially covered by a shrub, and David thanked God under his breath. He moved slowly, careful not to make any sudden movements, and crept towards the cave.

The opening was small but so was David. Once inside, his

eyes adjusted to the darkness, and he could see the cave was larger than anticipated. He ran deep into the mountainside and breathed a sigh of relief as he made his way further into the darkness. He held on to the cave's wall, scaling it with both hands, taking care not to fall. He came upon a clearing where light shone through from a small opening above.

David could still faintly hear their voices. Should he walk on, deeper into the cave? No. He needed the light. So he sat where he was, legs crossed on the rock beneath him. He waited and listened. If they saw the cave's opening, he'd be found. If he was found, he would be killed.

It had been so long now, so many months of running and hiding. He was tired of living in fear. His heart ached at the thought of a comfortable bed or a warm meal, just the memory of feeling safe and having peace. He was desperate for the chase to end.

David felt the familiar tug in his spirit and he closed his eyes. He smiled to himself, welcoming God's reassurance. It came over him gently at first, seeping in and clearing away his feelings of despair. God reminded David that he was not alone.

David reached back inside his pouch and wrapped his fingers around his scroll. He would write to him. To the only one who had any power over David's situation.

David felt close to God when he spoke with him by way of writing. Using the little light provided from above, David began.

O Lord, rescue me from evil people.
Protect me from those who are violent, those who plot
evil in their hearts and stir up trouble all day long…
O Lord, keep me out of the hands of the wicked.
Protect me from those who are violent,
for they are plotting against me.

The proud have set a trap to catch me; they have stretched
out a net; they have placed traps all along the way…
But I know the Lord will help those they persecute;
he will give justice to the poor.

David leaned back against the rock and closed his eyes.
He held his breath, listening, and peered up at the hole in the
roof above, but he could no longer hear their voices. So he
took his pen back to his scroll.

The familiar presence of his protector surrounded him,
filling the space where he sat. His hand took to the paper as
though it had a life of its own, and David knew he no longer
wrote alone. The words were not his own. They flowed easily,
and he let them come.

O Lord, you have examined my heart
and know everything about me.
You know when I sit down or stand up.
You know my thoughts even when I'm far away.
You see me when I travel and when I rest at home.
You know everything I do.
You know what I am going to say even before I say it,
Lord.
You go before me and follow me.
You place your hand of blessing on my head…
I can never escape from your Spirit!
I can never get away from your presence!
If I go up to heaven, you are there;
if I go down to the grave, you are there.
If I ride the wings of the morning, if I dwell by the
farthest oceans, even there your hand will guide me,
and your strength will support me…

You made all the delicate, inner parts of my body
and knit me together in my mother's womb.
Thank you for making me so wonderfully complex!
Your workmanship is marvellous – how well I know it.
You watched me as I was being formed in utter seclusion,
as I was woven together in the dark of the womb.
You saw me before I was born. Every day of my life was
recorded in your book. Every moment was laid out before
a single day had passed.

David dropped the pen and read through the words he had written as though reading them for the first time. His eyes welled with tears and they ran down his cheeks onto the scroll. He took his grubby hand and wiped them from his face.

David was loved. That he could be sure of, even if nothing else seemed to make sense. He didn't understand why he was being hunted, and he didn't understand why Saul wanted him dead. But none of that mattered as long as he remembered that he could trust in his God.

God reminded David again that he had a plan for David's life. God would help him.

(Psalm 140:1-2, 4-5, 12; Psalm 139:1-5, 7-10, 13-16)

Ziza

Ziza was late! She lifted her skirts and walked quickly towards the venue. She could hear the music well before she arrived – the celebration was already in full swing.

Ziza burst through the kitchen door and almost knocked over a tray of food held by Abitha, her boss. Abitha didn't have to say anything to Ziza – her disapproving look said enough. Instead, she handed Ziza the tray and pointed her straight back out the door to serve the gathered guests.

'Where have you been?' Ziza recognised Eden's voice hissing from behind her. 'We've been run off our feet, and Abitha's furious.'

'I know. I lost track of time,' Ziza said.

'Is that what we're calling it these days?' Eden winked at her. Ziza blushed. She hoped everyone didn't know why she was late. She was excited about her relationship with Joey and had wanted to tell somebody … but now she regretted confiding in Eden.

'I'm sorry,' she called after Eden. Abitha stepped out from the kitchen, and Ziza got to work. Head down and tail up, she made her way around the room, offering the guests delicacies from her platter.

Ziza's parents would be at the wedding, and she was worried Abitha might speak with her father. He'd be furious if he learned she'd been late.

She smiled at the guests as she served them, all the while racking her brain for an excuse for her father … in case she needed one. It wasn't even that her father would disapprove of her relationship with Joey. Joey was a good man, but they hadn't found the right time to tell their families yet. And for things to go smoothly, her parents must not hear about Joey from anybody else. It must come from her.

Ziza calmed as the hours went by. Her father was in good spirits, no doubt enjoying the wine. She could hear his belly laugh from across the room. Ziza's feet were tired. She was due for a break, but there was no way she was asking for one. She would wait until Abitha offered, otherwise she would work right through. So far, Abitha hadn't spoken with her parents – Ziza had kept an eye on them all evening.

It was getting late, and Ziza was giving up on the idea of a break when Eden popped up beside her.

'Abitha said you can take a break now.'

'Great. My feet are killing me.' Ziza placed her tray down on a table and followed Eden to the kitchen.

Abitha was there, in hushed conversation with a group of women. Ziza's heart sank to see that her mother was one of them.

'Girls, come here,' Abitha called them over. They hurried across the kitchen and Ziza braced herself.

'We have a problem,' Abitha said. 'There is no more wine.'

Thank goodness the discussion wasn't about her. But how embarrassing for the bride's family. It was too early for the celebration to end.

'I can help.' A woman beside Ziza's mother spoke up. Abitha raised her eyebrows.

'How will you help, Mary?' Abitha asked. It was more of a statement than a question, and Mary ignored her.

'Come with me,' Mary told Ziza and Eden.

'Ziza's on a break,' Eden said, 'but I'll come and help.' All eyes were on Ziza, and she saw her opportunity to get back in Abitha's good books.

'That's okay. I'll help too.' She ignored her grumbling stomach and aching feet. Abitha nodded her approval as the girls followed the older woman.

How would Mary help? Maybe they would accompany her home to pick up some wine. But she'd have to fetch an awful lot. Otherwise, it wouldn't go very far with so many wedding guests. Mary moved fast for an older woman, and Ziza and Eden hurried to keep up.

Ziza was surprised when Mary stopped just outside the front door. Tables were set up for the overflow of guests, who were eating, drinking, and enjoying themselves. Mary approached a group of young men at a table, and Ziza and Eden stood close behind her.

'Hello, Mother,' one of the men said. Mary sat beside her son.

'They have no more wine,' Mary told him quietly. A knowing look passed between them. Perhaps he owned a vineyard. Or perhaps he was extremely wealthy.

'Dear woman.' He shook his head. 'That's not our problem. My time has not yet come.'

Mary stood, apparently ignoring her son's response.

'Do whatever he tells you,' she said to Ziza and Eden. With that she was off again, back inside the house.

This was awkward. Ziza looked from Eden to the man still seated beside his friends. What should they do? It was obvious he didn't want to help.

Mary's son watched his mother as she entered the house, then stood. He turned his attention to the girls and smiled.

He looked around the yard, and pointed to the large stone water jars used for ceremonial washing.

'Fill the jars with water,' he said. Ziza was confused, but she and Eden nodded in response and turned to do as he'd asked.

'Is he crazy or something?' Eden hissed as they walked away.

'It's a possibility,' Ziza whispered back. The girls got to work, filling the jars with water. It was a lot of work, and such a waste of time. After all, it was wine that was needed, not water. When the jars were finally full, Ziza and Eden returned to the table where Mary's son sat.

'The jars are full,' Eden said. He nodded.

'Now, dip some out, and take it to the master of ceremonies.'

Ziza and Eden stood speechless and stunned as his words settled in. He rejoined the conversation with his friends, leaving the girls gaping at one another.

Ziza and Eden sped back to the water jars where they could speak in private.

'He is definitely crazy.' Eden threw her hands up in the air. 'We can't serve water to the master of the ceremonies. What will he think?'

'Wouldn't it be better to admit the wine has run out?' Ziza whispered. She stared into the water jars, torn as to what she should do. It was turning out to be an unusual evening.

'He's watching us,' Eden whispered. Ziza looked over at Mary's son, who looked cool and calm as he smiled at the girls.

Ziza waved awkwardly. She grabbed a cup from the table beside her, dipped it in the barrel of water, filled it to the brim, and raised it towards Mary's son. He nodded, still smiling to himself. Ziza couldn't be sure, but he seemed to be enjoying this.

The girls headed inside to find the master of the ceremonies. Ziza was embarrassed – the whole thing seemed foolish – but she needed to obey. She would deliver the drink then duck back to the kitchen as fast as she could.

The master of ceremonies was seated in the place of honour. Ziza was disappointed. She'd hoped they mightn't be able to find him. She paused and looked at Eden, then took a deep breath and approached the head table. She offered the cup to the master of ceremonies.

He took it straight to his lips, and the girls turned to leave.

'Excuse me.' The master of the ceremonies stopped them mid-step. Ziza's heart sank. What would they say now? How would they explain there was no more wine, only water? Ziza kept her eyes low, watching the ground at his feet.

'Fetch me the bridegroom,' he said. Ziza and Eden ran to deliver his request. They were back within minutes with the bridegroom by their side. The men greeted one another.

'A host always serves the best wine first,' the master of the ceremonies said.

Ziza held her breath. How would the bridegroom react?

'Then, when everyone has had a lot to drink, the host brings out the less expensive wine,' he continued. Ziza waited. It was obvious he wanted the rest of the wine … not water.

'But you have kept the best until now!'

The master of the ceremonies patted the bridegroom on the back before taking another sip from his cup. The bridegroom grinned from ear to ear.

'Come on,' Ziza whispered and ran back outside to the large water barrels. The girls checked all six, one by one. They were no longer full to the brim with water, but with wine.

The next day there was a wedding celebration in the village of Cana in Galilee. Jesus' mother was there, and Jesus and his disciples were also invited to the celebration. The wine supply ran out during the festivities, so Jesus' mother told him, 'They have no more wine.'

'Dear woman, that's not our problem,' Jesus replied. 'My time has not yet come.'

But his mother told the servants, 'Do whatever he tells you.'

Standing nearby were six stone water jars, used for Jewish ceremonial washing. Each could hold twenty to thirty gallons. Jesus told the servants, 'Fill the jars with water.' When the jars had been filled, he said, 'Now dip some out and take it to the master of ceremonies.' So the servants followed his instructions.

When the master of the ceremonies tasted the water that was now wine, not knowing where it had come from (though, of course, the servants knew), he called the bridegroom over. 'A host always serves the best wine first,' he said. 'Then, when everyone has had a lot to drink, he brings out the less expensive wine. But you have kept the best until now!' (John 2:1-10)

The Curtain

It was silent and still in the room and the curtain stood high and tall. The air was stale, and the room was peaceful – not a sound could be heard, not a soul was in sight. The presence of God was thick beyond the curtain, in the space he occupied, where he lived and breathed. The space no ordinary man could enter.

A holy space.

The curtain itself was large and heavy – sixty feet long and thirty feet wide. It was four inches thick. And its colour – a beautiful purple with scarlet and blue. The curtain was not easily shifted – it took three hundred men just to move it.

The curtain was important because it separated humanity from God. He was on one side, the creator of the universe. On the other was humanity, those he had created. Because of their many sins, humanity could not approach their creator. The curtain was a barrier, a divider between him and humanity. A symbol of separation.

And today was a day like any other in the quiet, peaceful room where the curtain hung unmovable and solemn, like a whisper of a warning. Tiny specks of dust floated through the air. The room became dark, as though a great shadow had been cast over its walls.

God watched as they killed his only son. Humanity nailed him to a cross and then looked on in delight as he struggled to breathe. His life was given for them. In the moment his breathing ceased, God turned to the curtain in the stillness of the room and he tore it. A mighty rip as the curtain split in two from the top right down to the bottom.

God destroyed the barrier separating himself from humanity. The symbol of separation was ripped apart by the sacrifice of his son. In that heart-wrenching moment, instead of punishing humanity, he forgave them. He was reunited with them, with his creation.

Jesus reunited the Father of the universe with the world he had created.

Then Jesus shouted out again, and he released his spirit. At that moment, the curtain in the sanctuary of the Temple was torn in two, from top to bottom. The earth shook, rocks split apart. (Matthew 27:50-51)

Tarah

Tarah had tried to stay away from Lachy, but he'd kissed her! And now she couldn't stay away. She was drawn to him like no other, even though she knew how wrong it was. She understood the risk she was taking.

Lachy was married and Tarah loved him. She'd watched him and thought about him and obsessed over him for close to a year, always assuming he felt nothing for her. He was married. Of course he didn't!

But then yesterday happened. Tarah had been washing up after dinner, and he had stopped to speak with her. It was clear he'd been drinking, but it was the festival of the shelters, so everyone else had been drinking too. Lachy had chatted and laughed with her, and it was just on dark when he'd shocked her by pushing her up against the wall and kissing her.

It hadn't just been any kiss either. There had been promise behind his kiss, promise of more to come. And Tarah wanted more.

She didn't think of Berry, Lachy's wife. Tarah and Berry had been friends since childhood, but Tarah told herself that Berry was obviously not keeping Lachy happy. And Tarah intended to.

She would go to his home, wait for Berry to leave then knock on his door. It was a brave thing to do. Tarah tried not to think about her parents or her family or anything else. All she thought about was Lachy's kiss and the way that it had made her feel.

Tarah walked the streets, heading towards Lachy's home, when she rounded a bend and spotted Berry. Her heart jumped into her throat. Berry had already left the house. Did that mean Lachy was home alone? Berry held her young son's hand as they walked together, heading into town. Good. They would be gone a while.

Tarah pushed aside her guilt and let her excitement take hold. She picked up her pace and almost skipped the rest of the short distance to his home, right up to Lachy's door.

She paused for only a second. It would be best if she wasn't seen entering Berry's home while she was out. Tarah stepped inside and spotted Lachy straight away. He stood in the courtyard, facing her, with his head down. Alone. Tarah didn't say anything, but she froze and watched him. He was gorgeous. Her heartbeat quickened. Lachy glanced up and did a double take when he saw Tarah. They stood in silence, their eyes locked.

Lachy grinned at her and moved the hair back from his face, tucking it behind his ear. It was a mischievous grin and Tarah's heart raced. Then, without a word, they crossed the courtyard, closing the gap between them and holding each other in a passionate embrace. When they kissed, the electricity from the night before shot through Tarah's body and she was pleased she had come. Lachy kissed Tarah's neck and nibbled at her ear.

'We don't have long,' he whispered. Tarah knew this was a point of no return … but she couldn't have stopped even if she'd wanted to. She let Lachy lead her into his sleeping room where he pushed her down to the bed, then joined her.

Less than a minute later, there was a noise from the door-way of the room. Tarah froze when she saw Jeb, Berry's older brother, standing in the doorway. Jeb looked from Lachy to Tarah in shock then disgust.

He strode into the room, grabbed hold of Tarah's arm, and yanked her up from the bed. She cried out in pain.

'It wasn't me, man,' Lachy said as Jeb pulled her from the room. 'She kissed me. I didn't even want to, I swear.' Lachy's words cut like a knife. She was alone now. All alone. This was on her.

Fear caught hold of her and made her lightheaded. She had been caught. They had been caught. She knew the punishment for adultery.

'Please, no!' She tried to pull her arm free from Jeb's grip. He didn't listen but yanked her even harder. She screamed and tears fell from her cheeks. They would kill her for this. She was eighteen years old and she would die today. Bile rose inside her and she held her free hand over her mouth as her feet pounded the earth beneath her. She couldn't hold the vomit, and it spilt through her fingers, over her tunic and onto the ground.

'You're disgusting.' Jeb turned to her. His eyes were on fire, and she knew he wasn't talking about the vomit.

The streets were filling with people and they watched as she was dragged into town. They stopped and stared.

'Jeb, please stop,' Tarah sobbed. 'It was a mistake, it won't happen again. I promise.'

'You have dishonoured my sister and you will pay the price.'

What would Tarah's parents think? How would her mother survive this? How would Tarah sit still and let them stone her to death?

She trembled from head to toe as Jeb dragged her up the steps of the temple, stopping before the Pharisees and teachers of religious law. Tarah searched their faces, looking for someone she knew, for someone who might help her. But there was no one.

Jeb spoke to the men in hushed voices. They looked over his shoulder at Tarah, their expressions showing disgust. Then they were off again, dragging Tarah further into the temple. She tried not to think about the rocks that would hit her face and her head. She wanted to live. It wasn't fair.

Or … was it? What had she done? What had she been thinking?

There was a crowd gathered in the temple, listening to a teacher. Jeb marched right up to the front of the crowd and pulled Tarah to stand facing them all. He finally let go of her arm. She covered her face with both hands and cried.

'Show them your face,' Jeb ordered.

Tarah looked up at the sea of faces before her. They would be hurting her soon. She had seen these things happen before. The crowd would help kill her when they discovered what she had done.

The Pharisees and teachers of religious law stood behind Jeb, tall and self-righteous.

'Ask Jesus,' one of them whispered to Jeb. Jeb turned to the man who had been teaching the crowd.

'Teacher,' Jeb said to Jesus. 'This woman was caught in the act of adultery.' The people in the crowd gasped and shook their heads at Tarah. 'The law of Moses says to stone her. What do you say?' Jeb asked.

Tarah's life hung on the teacher's reply. But why were they asking for his advice? Everyone knew what her punishment would be. Tarah held her breath, trembling uncontrollably.

Instead of answering Jeb, Jesus knelt down and used his finger to write in the dust at his feet.

Tarah's eyes flooded with tears and she couldn't make out what he was writing. She sensed the frustration in Jeb and the leaders.

'Well?' Jeb demanded. 'Are you going to answer me? Should we stone her?'

Tarah clenched her hands together. Jesus stood to his feet.

'All right,' he said to Jeb, and Tarah's heart dropped at his words. 'But let the one who has never sinned throw the first stone.'

Tarah couldn't believe her ears. What was this man saying? Since when did stoning someone become about having a clear conscience?

Jesus dropped back down to the ground and continued to write in the dust. What was he writing? Was he listing names…?

She didn't look at the men who accused her. Instead she kept her eyes to the ground and waited as the tears dropped from her chin onto her tunic. She didn't look, but she heard their footsteps as, one by one, the Pharisees and the teachers of religious law walked away until only Jeb remained. She could see his feet beside her. Finally, he sighed and left as well.

Tarah let out the breath she'd been holding. She lifted her hands back up to her face and then fell to her knees beside Jesus, weeping.

'Where are your accusers?' Jesus said.

He was speaking to Tarah now. She looked up into his eyes and was shocked at the compassion she saw in them. Did Jesus not find Tarah revolting like everyone else?

'Didn't even one of them condemn you?' he asked.

Tarah's hands still shook uncontrollably. 'No, Lord.'

Jesus reached out and took her hands in one of his. He looked her in the eyes, a look that somehow said he could see her and everything she had done and everything she had intended to do.

'Neither do I,' he said. His words shocked Tarah, and she looked at him, speechless and sorry for what she had done. He rose, held out his hand, and helped Tarah up from the ground.

'Go and sin no more.'

As he was speaking, the teachers of religious law and the Pharisees brought a woman who had been caught in the act of adultery. They put her in front of the crowd.

'Teacher,' they said to Jesus, 'this woman was caught in the act of adultery. The law of Moses says to stone her. What do you say?'

They were trying to trap him into saying something they could use against him, but Jesus stooped down and wrote in the dust with his finger. They kept demanding an answer, so he stood up again and said, 'All right, but let the one who has never sinned throw the first stone!' Then he stooped down again and wrote in the dust.

When the accusers heard this, they slipped away one by one, beginning with the oldest, until only Jesus was left in the middle of the crowd with the woman. Then Jesus stood up again and said to the woman, 'Where are your accusers? Didn't even one of them condemn you?'

'No, Lord,' she said.

And Jesus said, 'Neither do I. Go and sin no more.'
(John 8:3-11)

Nebo

Nebo sat on the roadside, letting the sun warm his skin. He spread his fingers out over the dirt and collected smooth stones. He liked to play with the stones in the palms of his hands during the long days.

Begging had been slow today. He'd heard familiar voices chatting among themselves as they walked by.

Sometimes he would give the voices a face in his imagination and would guess what their names might be. On the odd occasion, he would hear a name spoken as the people passed. On more than one occasion he had guessed correctly. He felt immense satisfaction on those days.

Most of his days were both long and lonely. He knew hunger well, and the heat was his constant companion.

As the sun moved throughout the day, Nebo would scale the wall he leaned against, familiar nooks and footholds helping him find his way.

He would move until he came across small alcoves of shaded space where he could rest before the sun found him and beat down on his head once again.

Nebo had been born blind and knew no different, only the world inside his head.

He often pondered his blindness, why others could see while he lived in darkness. He would imagine what he might have done if his eyes had been whole. The life he might have lived.

It was early afternoon, and Nebo held a smooth stone in

his palm. He turned it around, over and over again. Voices approached, but they were not familiar voices. He listened, leaning his head back against the stone wall.

'Rabbi, why was this man born blind? Was it because of his own sins or his parents' sins?'

Nebo held his breath. Who were these people? Who was this rabbi? And what answer would he give for the question of Nebo's heart?

'It was not because of his sins or his parents' sins,' another voice replied. The rabbi?

Nebo dropped the stone to the ground and stretched out his hand towards the men. He yearned to speak to this rabbi.

'Then why, Rabbi?'

'This happened so the power of God could be seen in him,' the voice of the rabbi said. 'We must quickly carry out the tasks assigned us by the one who sent us. The night is coming and then no one can work. But while I am here in the world, I am the light of the world'.

A shiver ran down Nebo's spine, and his head spun. He might have fallen over if he hadn't already been seated. The power of God, the light of the world … what did this rabbi mean?

Nebo was drawn to his voice. He reached his hands out further, following the direction of their voices.

Suddenly a hand touched Nebo's. The fingers wrapped around Nebo's outstretched hand. Human touch was not a regular part of Nebo's life. He clutched the hand and held it tight. Nebo instinctively knew the hand belonged to the man they called 'Rabbi'.

The rabbi pulled Nebo up until he stood. Still holding Nebo's hand, the rabbi brushed the hair from Nebo's forehead. He pushed it back, clear of his eyes.

He then let go of Nebo's hand and stooped down before him. Nebo could hear him spit onto the ground and heard his hands running over the dirt at their feet. He knew this sound well.

The rabbi stood back up and held Nebo's head between his hands. He used his thumbs to spread the wet mud, smearing it over Nebo's eyelids. It felt smooth and smelled of earth.

Nebo was both shocked and intrigued. Words escaped him. The human touch alone was powerful enough, but Nebo could feel that the very presence of this man was something else.

Nebo longed to stay with him, to feel his hands against his face, to hear his voice again.

Nebo's eyelids felt heavy with the wet dirt.

'Go wash yourself in the pool of Siloam,' the rabbi said.

Nebo scaled the wall, following the familiar road. He knew his way well. He had visited the pool many times, although never had his face been full of mud or his heart so full of life. *Go and wash yourself in the pool of Siloam.* The rabbi's words played in his mind.

He didn't know what to make of it, where to even start making sense of this day. His chest burnt with the rabbi's words, as though it were on fire. He could feel the mud drying on his eyelids and held back the urge to rub it off. He would follow the rabbi's instructions. He would wait to wash it away in the pool.

Nebo leaned down beside the pool. He could sense others watching, but he didn't care. He reached down using both hands to cup the water and splash it up over his face. He repeated this, over and over, until he could feel the mud had been washed away. He sat back beside the pool and used the palms of his hands to wipe the water from his eyes.

When Nebo opened his eyes, he could see his hands for the first time in his life.

Then he spit on the ground, made mud with the saliva, and spread the mud over the blind man's eyes. He told him, 'Go wash yourself in the pool of Siloam.' So the man went and washed and came back seeing! (John 9:6-7)

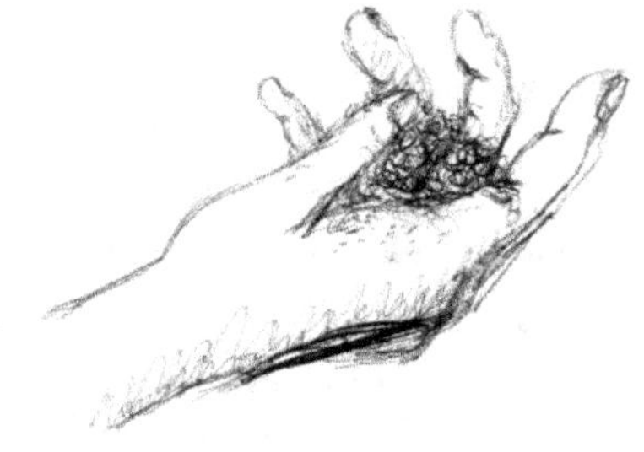

Mary

Mary was in shock. It had happened fast, and in a stable of all places!

Joseph slept beside her, stretched out on the hay. She sat awake, watching her baby lying in the makeshift bed, wrapped in strips of cloth. She felt elated as though she were in a dream.

Childbirth had been more painful than she'd anticipated. She'd cried out and rocked back and forth, swaying over the hay beneath her.

There had been a time towards the end when she'd wanted to give up, wondering if she'd survive. But he had drawn near to her then, as though whispering and reassuring her. And somewhere in the throes of her anguish, she'd remembered whose baby she carried.

Now she could not take her eyes off of him. She leaned close, watching his face. He was perfect, with his lips so red and his skin so clear.

She had wondered who he would look like. Would he resemble her? She guessed he wouldn't look like Joseph. Was it possible he would look like his Father? It was hard to wrap her head around it.

Mary lifted him, cradling him to her chest, and tiptoed to the barn door.

She sat carefully on a pile of hay, with the moon and stars

before her, holding her face close to his. She looked up at the stars and her eyes welled with tears.

'Your son,' she whispered. 'Thank you.'

She gave birth to her first child, a son. She wrapped him snugly in strips of cloth and laid him in a manger, because there was no lodging available for them. (Luke 2:7)

Two Thousand Years Later

'Listen.' Gamaliel spoke once, and the men grew silent. He was well respected and brought a lifetime of wisdom and a wealth of experience. He'd spent long enough sitting in the corner listening to their arguments back and forth.

'Settle, men. Calm yourselves,' he spoke again. All eyes were now on him. He let the silence sit in the room for a moment before continuing.

'Now think about this. Think clearly. We've seen this type of thing happen before. A rebel rises up and forms a following.' Gamaliel scanned the room and saw blank stares all round.

'But when we have the rebel killed, what happens to his followers?' he asked.

Gamaliel watched as understanding settled over the expressions of the teachers gathered in the room.

'That's right,' he nodded. 'Take away their leader, and the followers fall away too.' There were hushed whispers and relieved faces around the room.

'No one will remember his name in a month or so. Don't get ahead of yourselves. There's no need to get worked up. Be wise, men.'

Gamaliel turned to sit back down in his corner then turned back to face the teachers as a second thought struck him. 'And if by some miracle they do remember his name, if his followers don't go away… then perhaps Jesus really was the son of God.'

But one member, a Pharisee named Gamaliel, who was an expert in religious law and respected by all the people, stood up and ordered that the men be sent outside the council chamber for a while. Then he said to his colleagues, "Men of Israel, take care what you are planning to do to these men! Some time ago there was that fellow Theudas, who pretended to be someone great. About 400 others joined him, but he was killed, and all his followers went their various ways. The whole movement came to nothing. After him, at the time of the census, there was Judas of Galilee. He got people to follow him, but he was killed, too, and all his followers were scattered.

'So my advice is, leave these men alone. Let them go. If they are planning and doing these things merely on their own, it will soon be overthrown. But if it is from God, you will not be able to overthrow them. You may even find yourselves fighting against God!' (Acts 5:34-39)

Jojo

Jojo stood looking at the linen, but his mind was somewhere else – on a hill, with the one who he believed had been the Son of God. Tears sprang to his eyes and the store owner approached him

'Can I help you, sir?' she asked.

'Yes.' Jojo cleared his throat. 'I need some linen, the finest you have.'

'How much would you like?' she asked.

'It's for a burial.' Joseph kept his eyes downcast. 'I'll need a large piece.' His voice broke, and the woman who served him touched his arm. She held her hand there for a moment before she got busy fulfilling his request.

It was more difficult to take his body down from the cross than Jojo had imagined. But he managed, with the help of four other men. Jojo wrapped him in the large piece of linen he'd bought. Now he stood to the side, watching as his body lay in the arms of his mother. She cried bitterly and held her face against his, kissing him and whispering in his ear. It was hard to watch. Jojo understood she needed this time. It was precious time.

The blood-stained nails were at Jojo's feet and he knelt to pick one up. The iron was cool against his palm. He turned it over and shuddered at the thought of it piercing through flesh. He placed it back beside the others. On second thoughts, he gathered them all up and carefully placed them inside his bag. He wasn't sure why, but he wanted to keep them.

Jojo approached Jesus' mother, inviting her to come with them. Together they left the hill, the place where Jesus had been murdered. They carried his body with them to Jojo's tomb, which had been carved out of the rock. Jojo had expected to lie in this tomb himself someday. The tomb was cool and dark inside. Their small party was silent as they laid his body down.

Jojo felt the significance of the moment but there were no words. Instead, he held in his heart the words that could not be expressed. He was gone. Their teacher, healer, leader, son, and friend. He had been unable to save himself. Jojo had hoped, had believed, he would. Somehow. But Jojo had been wrong. Not even Jesus could stand against the Roman Empire.

A large, heavy stone was rolled across the entrance of the tomb, sealing it permanently shut. As Jojo left, he turned back one last time. She was still there, his mother, sitting outside the tomb. Jojo could just make out her shadow in the moonlight. Maybe she would stay all night. Jojo took a deep breath. He had done all he could now, and he was tired.

He turned and walked home.

Joseph of Arimathea took a risk and went to Pilate and asked for Jesus' body. (Joseph was an honored member of the high council, and he was waiting for the Kingdom of God to come.)

Pilate couldn't believe that Jesus was already dead, so he called for the Roman officer and asked if he had died yet. The officer confirmed that Jesus was dead, so Pilate told

Joseph he could have the body. Joseph bought a long sheet of linen cloth. Then he took Jesus body down from the cross, wrapped it in the cloth, and laid it in a tomb that had been carved out of the rock. Then he rolled a stone in front of the entrance. Mary Magdalene and Mary the mother of Joseph saw where Jesus' body was laid. (Mark 15:43-47)

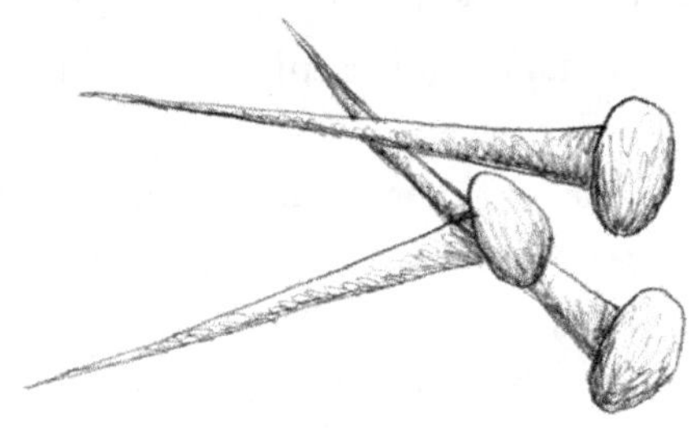

Dotty

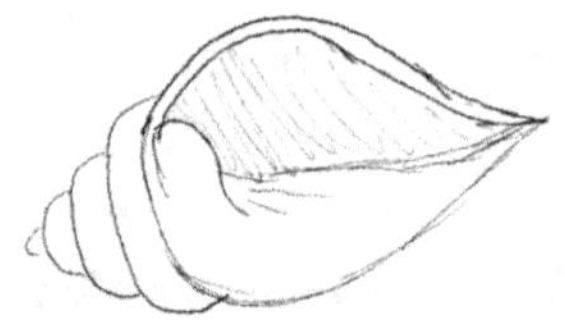

Dotty walked along the shoreline of a heavenly beach. It was much like the beaches she'd known on earth, only more peaceful and breathtakingly beautiful. And this beach was completely secluded.

She walked alone with her thoughts and felt his love surrounding her even now, when all alone. She was never unsure of his presence anymore. It was thick, like a blanket that wrapped itself around her no matter where she wandered.

He'd brought her here to show her something, but she did not know what. She sensed she needed to keep walking. The water lapped at her feet, warm and refreshing, when Dotty spotted something written in the sand. She stooped down to see what it was. It was his name written in the sand, the letters spelled out in a familiar way *J-e-s-u-s*.

The word took her back to her life, to the hundreds of times she'd taken a shell to the sand and spelled his name out just like this.

On closer inspection, Dotty realised his name was written in her own handwriting. Her distinctive *J* gave it away. Dotty was confused; she certainly hadn't written this. What did it mean? She stood and eyeballed the sand message, trying to figure it out, but she didn't know, so she continued walking.

Before long, she came upon another message in the sand, again in her handwriting.

Jesus loves you.

She looked further down the beach. There were more and more messages. Sometimes his name stood alone, while other times the message was about his love.

The messages were Dotty's. She remembered the countless times she'd written in the sand during her days on earth, sometimes on stormy days when the beach was secluded and sometimes when the sun shone bright. But always for him.

And here she was now, on a beach in heaven, and it was clear that he had seen her messages. He'd collected the messages she'd written in the sand in all her years on earth. He'd collected them and laid them out on his own beach and showed them to her now. Her messages had meant something to him.

She saw faces then, glimpses of those he had brought across her sand messages. Of the way he had used her words to reach people. People who needed to hear the words, 'Jesus loves you', even if the words were only written on a lonely stormy beach.

He'd been involved in every detail of her life. He'd watched even the workings of her fingertips. She hadn't known he'd been so close.

She hadn't known just how much he thought about her.

How precious are your thoughts about me, O God.
They cannot be numbered!
I can't even count them;
they outnumber the grains of sand!
And when I wake up, you are still with me!
(Psalm 139:17-18)

Jet

Jet was sure it would be a couple of boring days ahead. He'd been stationed to guard a dead man's tomb. It seemed like a waste of time. Were they afraid he would up and escape? It was laughable!

Jet had seen the criminal himself. He'd been tortured and was well and truly dead. There was talk the authorities were worried his friends – they called themselves disciples – would try to steal his body. Jet thought that sounded ridiculous too, but it didn't matter what he thought. He just had to obey orders and do as he was told.

So here he was, standing outside a tomb, guarding a dead man for three days. A large rock covered the tomb's entrance, for which Jet was thankful. It was the end of day two and there would be a stench by now. Chip stood beside him, looking out to the twilight sky.

The two guards had talked about so much over the past couple of days, out of sheer boredom. Jet had never liked Chip. He'd thought he was conceited and opinionated. But he had found the last two days getting to know him surprisingly pleasant. Jet knew he could be judgmental and suspected he'd judged Chip prematurely.

'Well, that was another quiet day at the gravesite.' Jet winked and Chip chuckled.

'Yes, it sure was. It seems the dead man is still dead.'

'What a surprise.' The men took turns to eat dinner at dusk while the other stood watch before the tomb.

'I'll take the first shift tonight,' Jet said. There was no protest from Chip, who was soon fast asleep.

As the night grew darker, Jet found it hard to keep his eyes open. He leaned back against the rock that covered the tomb's entrance. It was a huge rock and must have taken many men to move it.

He leant his head back, resting it against the rock, and closed his eyes. He would rest them, just for a minute or so …

A cow bellowed in the distance, and he woke with a start. He needed to stay awake. He slapped his cheeks and stood straight, off the rock, and looked up to the night sky. The sky was filled with stars and he counted them. He counted them for hours until finally it was his turn to sleep.

It was Sunday morning now. Jet and Chip stood side by side before the tomb, ready to face their third and final day of guard duty. There was movement ahead, but it was too early to see clearly enough to make out who was there. The men stood to attention.

'It could be his disciples,' Chip whispered. Jet strained his eyes, trying to see who was approaching.

'Who goes there?' Jet called out.

'It is Mary,' a woman's voice answered and Jet relaxed. The outlines of two women approached the tomb. It was the dead man's mother and another woman. They were no threat.

Suddenly without warning, the ground shifted beneath Jet, and he was thrown to the ground. Chip fell beside him, and the women cried out. Jet clutched the ground, trying to hold on to anything he could grasp. What was happening? Was it an earthquake? Jet covered his head with his arms to protect himself. The fierce shaking continued. It was so violent that the large stone covering the tomb was rolled away from the entrance. Jet and Chip scurried across the ground away from the stone. Just like that, the earth stopped trembling and was still.

Jet jumped to his feet, shaken and dazed, and Chip rose as well. There was a man sitting on top of the stone that had been rolled away. His face was bright, so bright that it seemed to shine like lightning, and Jet couldn't stand to look into it. The man's clothing was white, like snow. Jet gasped. Where had he come from? Was he human? Jet didn't think so … and the thought sent a shiver down his spine.

Jet was filled with fear and he trembled from head to toe. Chip fell beside him in a dead faint. Jet felt consciousness slipping away and he fell to the ground.

The next day, on the Sabbath, the leading priests and the Pharisees went to see Pilate. They told him, 'Sir, we remember what that deceiver once said while he was still alive: "After three days I will rise from the dead." So we request that you seal the tomb until the third day. This will prevent his disciples from coming and stealing his body and then telling everyone he was raised from the dead! If that happens, we'll be worse off than we were at first.'

Pilate replied, 'Take guards and secure it the best you can.' So they sealed the tomb and posted guards to protect it.

Early on Sunday morning, as the new day was dawning, Mary Magdalene and the other Mary went out to visit the tomb.

Suddenly there was a great earthquake! For an angel of

the Lord came down from heaven, rolled aside the stone, and sat on it…

The guards shook with fear when they saw him, and they fell into a dead faint.

Then the angel spoke to the women. 'Don't be afraid!' he said. 'I know you are looking for Jesus, who was crucified. He isn't here! He is risen from the dead, just as he said would happen…' (Matthew 27:62-66; Matthew 28:1-2, 4-6)

Iddo

Iddo the pig was four years old. He lived in a field on a farm with nine other pigs and a kind farmer who cared for them well. Iddo spent his days relaxing in the shade or basking in the hot sun and playing with the other pigs in his pen.

It was a good life, living on the farm. Iddo's favourite part of each day was feeding time. Iddo was always hungry and could eat fast, which worked out well for him during mealtimes.

But Iddo had a problem. It was a peculiar problem and until today, Iddo had been sure he must be mistaken, that it was all just in his head. But today the unthinkable had happened.

A new farmhand had been hired a few weeks earlier. Right from the beginning, something about the fellow had made Iddo uncomfortable. It was something about the way the man looked at their food. Iddo didn't like it.

Iddo reasoned with himself that he was being ridiculous. After all, Iddo was paranoid when it came to food. But as the days went by, Iddo became more and more concerned about the man's intentions. He looked at the pig food as though he wanted to eat it himself. Iddo didn't need anyone else to compete with when it came to mealtimes and he certainly did not want to share with a human.

Then he'd arrived with their food this morning. Iddo and the other pigs had run to their feeding trough as the farm-hand emptied their feed into it. Iddo ran faster than the other pigs and arrived first, burying his face deep in the food. He came up for air a minute later. Much to his surprise, the farmhand was kneeling beside him, his head also in their food. Iddo almost choked on his mouthful. What was going on here? Who was this man? And why was he eating pig food?

The man looked at Iddo, then sat back on his bottom, held his head in his hands, and cried. Iddo paused for only a second before burying his head back in the feed. He kept eating, pleased the human seemed to have had enough for now.

Iddo and the others devoured what was left. When the trough had been licked clean, Iddo sat back and watched the interesting man behind him.

The man still cried. Iddo burped.

The man looked up at Iddo for a few seconds before he laughed out loud and shook his head. Iddo stared at him.

'At home, even the hired servants have food enough to spare.' He seemed to be speaking to Iddo, which was unusual. 'And here I am dying of hunger!' He threw his hands up in the air.

There was a long pause, and Iddo stood to leave.

'I will go home to my father.' The farmhand sat up straight and nodded decidedly. 'I'll say, "Father, I have sinned against both heaven and you, and I am no longer worthy of being called your son. Please take me on as a hired servant."'

Iddo couldn't be sure, but it sounded like the farmhand might leave. That pleased Iddo. He didn't want to share any more of his food.

The man jumped to his feet, faster than Iddo had seen him move in all the weeks he'd been on the farm. He jumped the fence, too, and was gone without a second look back at Iddo or the farm.

Iddo hoped he would never come back again.

(Jesus told them this story to illustrate God's love for humanity.)

'A man had two sons. The younger son told his father, "I want my share of your estate now before you die." So his father agreed to divide his wealth between his sons.

'A few days later this younger son packed all his belongings and moved to a distant land, and there he wasted all his money in wild living. About the time his money ran out, a great famine swept over the land, and he began to starve. He persuaded a local farmer to hire him, and the man sent him into his fields to feed the pigs. The young man became so hungry that even the pods he was feeding the pigs looked good to him. But no one gave him anything.

'When he finally came to his senses, he said to himself, "At home even the hired servants have food enough to spare, and here I am dying of hunger! I will go home to my father and say, 'Father, I have sinned against both heaven and you, and I am no longer worthy of being called your son. Please take me on as a hired servant.'"

'So he returned home to his father. And while he was still a long way off, his father saw him coming. Filled with love and compassion, he ran to his son, embraced him, and kissed him.' (Luke 15:11-20)

Peter

Peter loved Jesus more than he loved anybody, yet somehow Peter had betrayed him. He sat alone in the corner of the room and held his head in his hands.

He hadn't been able to eat in three days. Not a bite. Not since that day.

Jesus had known it would happen. He'd looked Peter straight in the eyes and said, plain and simple, that Peter would deny him when Jesus needed him most. Just the thought of it sent another tear down Peter's face. It made him sick.

How could he have let this happen? How could he have betrayed his best friend? Peter wiped the tears from his cheeks with the back of his hand. His grief rolled in stages, and today he wanted to explode. He would never forgive himself.

Jesus had spoken incredible promises over Peter's life and Peter knew those promises were no longer his. He wasn't the man Jesus had hoped he was. Peter could imagine the disappointment in Jesus' eyes as though he sat before him now. He squeezed his temples with his forefingers. What was the point of anything anymore? How would he go on without Jesus? How would he ever come to terms with the fact that he had left Jesus for dead?

It had been three days now since they'd crucified Jesus, and Peter missed him. His guidance and reassurance had given Peter hope and something to live for. Without him, Peter's life was empty.

A hand touched Peter's shoulder, but he didn't look up. He hadn't heard anyone come in. He wanted to be alone, so he remained silent, eyes downcast and unresponsive. Hopefully whoever it was would get the hint and leave. But the hand didn't move. Instead, it held on to Peter's shoulder, firm and steady.

Peter opened his eyes and stared at the floor between his legs. It was dirty, and dust covered the ground around his sandals. A shiver ran down his spine. He had the oddest feeling that he knew who the hand belonged to, that he knew him well.

But that was ridiculous. There was no way. It couldn't be him … yet Peter was afraid to look up.

He heard the person standing beside him breathing in and out and in and out. Ever so slowly, Peter raised his head. He came face to face with Jesus. Peter jumped back, knocking over his chair. Fear and wonder fell over him as he gasped out loud.

'It's you!' Tears flooded over and spilled down Peter's cheeks.

'Yes, it's me,' Jesus said.

Peter leapt forward and wrapped his giant arms around his friend. He held Jesus tight, tighter than he'd ever held another. He wouldn't let him go. It was impossible, yet here he was. Alive. Standing before him, his tears wetting Peter's shoulder. His heart beat against Peter's.

He was alive.

'I'm so sorry.' Peter sobbed, remembering his betrayal. 'I'm so sorry'. The same words, over and over. Gut-wrenching words, truth from his very depths.

Jesus pulled away from Peter and looked him square in the eyes. 'I forgive you, my friend.'

With that, Peter dropped to the floor. He cried into his hands and Jesus sat beside him. Jesus leant his back against the wall and held his hand firmly on Peter's back.

And within the hour they were on their way back to Jerusalem. There they found the eleven disciples and the others who had gathered with them, who said, 'The Lord has really risen! He appeared to Peter.' (Luke 24:33-34)

Postscript

I didn't have a name for this collection of stories and the only people who ever heard them were my children. My thirteen-year-old daughter Milla had listened to them often.

One morning when we were on holiday in Hawaii, I asked God to help me find a title because I had no idea. Within an hour, the idea came to me that I could call my book 'Goldie'. I love this as a child's name but had never considered calling my stories by it. I wasn't sure if it was a silly idea or not, but something about the thought excited me.

Later that day, my daughter and I lay on the beach beside each other and, as I was resting/dozing, she chatted to me continuously. I was half listening.

She was talking about how she sees her life in colours – for example, she has a different colour for each year's classroom at school. Suddenly she asked me, 'What colour would your stories be Mum?'

I was still only half listening when I replied, 'I'm not sure, maybe rainbow.'

She thought about it for a couple of seconds before replying. 'No, they're gold Mum, definitely gold.'

Thank you for reading my stories through to the end. I hope you heard him whisper to you through the lines and the pages, and I hope you remembered that he sees you and knows your story.

That he listens to your words as you string together sentences and he watches your life with love-shaped eyes.

That when the cross weighed him down and he struggled to keep moving, he took another step because he thought of you.

He thought of your family, of your bloodline, of that beautiful familiarity you get when you step into your home and close the door to the world behind you.

Of your life.

He thought of you.

– Stacey